A SCORE TO SETTLE

CAZ FINLAY

One More Chapter
a division of HarperCollins*Publishers* Ltd
1 London Bridge Street
London SE1 9GF
www.harpercollins.co.uk
HarperCollins*Publishers*
Macken House, 39/40 Mayor Street Upper,
Dublin 1, D01 C9W8

This paperback edition 2023
1
First published in Great Britain in ebook format
by HarperCollins*Publishers* 2023

A catalogue record of this book is available from the British Library
ISBN: 978-0-00-854528-4

Printed and bound in the UK using 100% Renewable Electricity
by CPI Group (UK) Ltd

To all the readers who have loved Grace and the Carters – thank you for making my dreams come true.

And as always, for Eric and my boys x

Prologue

The girl's eyes were unmistakeable. The same deep blue as her father's – and her grandfather's too. A shiver ran the length of her spine as she remembered *him*. Their time together had been brief, but it had impacted her life so profoundly that she had never been the same again. He was the start of it all. The root of everything that had gone wrong in her life could be traced right back to him – and where he was, *she* would always be too. Between them, they had taken everything from her.

Everything!

And now this gift had been presented to her like an answer to all of her prayers. The little girl with the dark hair and the bright smile – sitting at her table and chattering about dolls and tea parties. She was a pretty little thing. Confident and well-spoken. The apple of her family's eye, no doubt. How much would they miss her if she didn't go home today? Would they wail and shriek and claw their fingernails down the walls? Would they drive themselves crazy wondering what had happened to her? Thinking about their beautiful child and how desperately she needed them? Imagining the worst possible things that could have happened? The pain. The anguish. The bone-deep, soul-wrenching fear of a parent not being able to protect their child. They were thoughts that never went away. An endless cycle of what ifs and if onlys.

She smiled as she talked to the little girl with the bright-blue eyes. They were going to get along so well, she just knew it. This beautiful, unblemished child was her compensation for all they had taken from her. She only wished she could be around to see their pain when their little light was taken from them. To see them fall apart the way that she had would be the icing on the cake.

But she had to be smart. She had to move quickly. No one would ever suspect her, but *she* would know who had taken their precious Isla.

She would know true pain – of the kind she had never imagined possible.

Chapter One

Milo Savage listened to the ringtone in his ear and cursed under his breath. John Barrow was avoiding him. This was the fourth time he'd called with no answer. The call went to voicemail.

'Fuck!' he muttered before he pressed the call button again. He was going to keep ringing the slimy little cunt until he picked up the phone. He might be in prison but Milo knew that he had access to a phone in his cell.

After several more rings, former Chief Superintendent John Barrow answered.

'Why the fuck are you avoiding me?' Milo snarled.

'I'm not avoiding you,' Barrow said with a patronising sigh. 'But in case you forgot, I'm in a jail cell here. I don't have the luxury of answering calls whenever I feel like it. I had to wait until the screws were out of earshot, didn't I?'

Milo bit back the retort on his tongue. JB was lying and he knew it. He'd been avoiding him like the plague since all of the shit went down with the Carters a few weeks earlier. 'Whatever,' he snapped. 'I need you to get me out of the country. You said you could make that happen. It's been three weeks and I'm still sitting here waiting. You're as useless as a fucking fart trapped in a bottle. You said you had connections.'

'I do,' JB snarled down the phone at him. 'But it's not quite so easy to make someone disappear when they have the biggest criminals in the North-West scouring the country looking for them, is it? If you hadn't fucked up...'

'*I* fucked up?' Milo spat as the anger burned in his chest. He took a deep breath before he spoke again. 'You were the one who recruited that pair of idiots to do the job,' he snarled, recalling the thick-as-fuck and, quite frankly, feral King brothers, who had murdered Glenda Alexander and were supposed to have framed Connor Carter for the crime. Instead they had messed up and her son, Danny, had been arrested instead. That wouldn't have been so bad, except the two of them fucked the whole thing up and one of them, Jerrod, was eventually arrested for the murder. The other brother, Devlin, did a runner, and hadn't been seen since. However, Milo had enough of an ear to the ground to suspect that Jake Conlon and the Carters had found the little rat and dispensed with him in their own particular way. And if he didn't get out of the fucking country soon, he'd be next.

'I handed you Conlon and the Carters on a fucking plate,' JB hissed down the phone. 'I never said the King brothers were candidates for *Mastermind*, I told you they were vicious little cunts who would do anything for a chance at some power. You were supposed to keep them in line, but you were more interested in running off with that whore.'

'Don't call her a whore,' Milo spat the words out. After all his years of waiting for her, Jasmine had rejected him. She claimed to be in love with Connor Carter, but Milo knew that wasn't true. It couldn't be. She loved *him*. They were meant to be together. He wouldn't have anyone calling her a whore and certainly not a piece of scum like John Barrow.

'That is exactly what she is and you know it,' Barrow said with a laugh and Milo squeezed the phone in his hand. He was seconds away from smashing it into the wall beside him, but, as much as he hated to admit it, he needed Barrow's help.

'Look. What about this move you promised me? I've been sitting in this fucking squat for weeks now. You get more fucking fresh air than I do.'

'I'm working on it, Milo,' JB snapped. 'I'm not a fucking magician. You have pissed off the entire North-West.'

'Just remember that I can make your life inside very uncomfortable, John,' Milo reminded him. The threat in his words was implicit. As a former copper now in prison, JB was hated by the prisoners and the screws, and it wouldn't take much for someone to turn on him some day. But if Milo were to tell Jake Conlon and Connor Carter that it was JB behind the plot to frame one of them for Glenda's murder, well, he wouldn't last the week.

'I already told you, I'm doing everything I can. You need to give me time.'

'I'm running out of time, fuck-nut!' Milo hissed. 'So get it done, because if I'm not out of the country by the end of the week, your cosy little cell in Strangeways won't be so cosy no more. You understand me?' With that Milo ended the call and threw the phone onto the sofa.

'Fuck!' he raged as he stomped around the tiny flat. He had to get out of there and fast. He'd been in prison for years and now that he was out he should be enjoying his freedom, not cooped up in a tiny one-bed in the bowels of Stoke. He fucking hated it. He felt like a sitting duck. He didn't trust Barrow one bit and was sure the slimy little prick would do him over if he had the chance, but Milo didn't have much choice. He didn't have many friends left now that he'd screwed over Jake Conlon and Connor Carter, but he did have JB over a barrel. He was a self-serving prick and he would do anything to save his own skin. The only way to stop Milo talking would be to get him out of the country like he'd promised to.

———

John Barrow lay back on his bunk in his cell and stared at the mobile phone in his hand. Milo Savage was a thorn in his side and one he needed to be rid of sooner rather than later. He had promised the man he could get him out of the country and he'd thought it would have been an easier job than it was turning out to be. The truth was, he didn't have the connections he once had, and it pained him to admit it. He was once a man who could get anything done, yet now he was scrabbling around for favours like a damn peasant. And all because that bitch Grace Carter had stuck her nose into police business and got herself involved in the investigation of some Liverpool prostitutes. Like anyone gave a shit about some missing whores. But saint fucking Grace liked to pretend that she was one of the people. That was why half of Liverpool fucking adored her, and the other half – well, they just shat their pants at the mention of her name.

She was sunning herself in the Costa del Sol while he was rotting in some filthy prison cell. It would be laughable if it wasn't so fucking depressing.

He placed the phone on the bunk beside him and sighed. He would have to forget about his vendetta with the Carters for now, at least until he could sort out his Milo problem. The easiest thing to do would be to just feed him to the sharks, but JB knew that as soon as anyone came near Milo, he would fold like a wet newspaper and throw JB straight under the bus. And while he didn't care much for Milo Savage, the man was shrewd and ruthless. He would do anything to save his own life and he wouldn't think twice about spilling his guts the second anyone harmed a hair on his head. And if the Carters did find out Barrow had been behind the recent goings-on, he knew he'd be a dead man walking. The very thought of their reach within prison made his sphincter clench.

He picked up his phone again and scrolled through the

stored numbers until he came to the one he was looking for. He pressed call and listened to the ringing sound while he waited for his former colleague to pick up.

'Why are you calling me?' DI Grosvenor said as soon as he answered the call.

'I'm calling to collect on my favour,' Barrow replied.

'You collected on that a few weeks ago, John, or have you forgotten already?'

Barrow smiled. Grosvenor was a good copper really, but John had dirt on him from years ago when he'd been a lowly constable. It was information that would ruin his career and his marriage in one fell swoop, and JB intended to use it to his advantage as often and for as long as he could. Grosvenor had been in charge of the investigation into Glenda Alexander's murder and he had overlooked some things, as he'd been asked to – nothing that would look too suspicious or dodgy, but it had been handy to have him as the Senior Investigating Officer on the case.

'I think we both know the information I have on you is worth way more than you overlooking a few discrepancies on a case, don't you?' JB asked.

'What the fuck do you want?' Grosvenor hissed down the phone.

'Your wife about, is she, Kevin? And what about them lovely little kiddies of yours?'

'Fuck you!' he snarled. 'I asked you what you want now.'

'I just need you to help me get a friend of mine out of the country is all,' Barrow replied.

'Who the fuck do you think I am, John? I can't get people out of the country.'

'I think you underestimate yourself, Grosvenor,' Barrow insisted. 'You're a smart man, I'm sure you could think of something. He only needs a passport, but they're so fucking difficult to get hold of these days.'

'You think I can get a fake passport?' Grosvenor scoffed.

'I think you'd better figure out a way to, Grosvenor, or your wife is going to find out why you both had to move from Wallasey to Liverpool all of those years ago.'

'You're an evil cunt,' Grosvenor snarled. 'You've held this over me for fourteen years, John. I'd have done less time if I'd actually been done for the crime.'

'Yeah, but you didn't, did you? That poor girl never walked again after what you did. I still have the pictures, Grosvenor, but they're safe. Don't worry,' he chuckled.

'Cunt!' Grosvenor snarled.

Barrow smiled. Grosvenor had been drunk as a skunk the night his wife had gone into labour with their eldest daughter. He'd jumped in his car and raced off down the road, only to wrap the car around a lamppost and a teenage girl on a bicycle a few hundred yards away. Fortunately for Grosvenor, Barrow had witnessed the entire thing and had covered it all up for him, disposing of the car, calling an ambulance for the victim and getting Grosvenor into a taxi to the hospital to witness the birth of his first-born. Barrow had taken some pictures on his mobile phone too, because even back then, he knew the importance of having something to hold over his colleagues.

'So, I can count on you to help me with my little problem, Kevin?' Barrow asked.

'As long as you swear this will be the last thing, John. This is enough now.'

'Of course,' Barrow agreed, even though he knew he'd call on Grosvenor's services again if he needed to. The thing with a lie was, the longer you covered it up, and the more you did to cover it up, the deeper you got and the worse the lie became. It was no longer just about the original incident fourteen years earlier – now it was about the lie that Grosvenor had told his wife for almost their entire marriage about what happened that night, the family who never got justice for the hit-and-run driver who almost killed their fifteen-year-old daughter and confined her to a wheelchair for the rest of her days, the murder investigation and the framing of an innocent man he'd been a party to – and now this.

With each new thing he did, Grosvenor became further indebted to him, not less.

'Who needs to leave the country?' Grosvenor asked with a resigned sigh.

'He'll be in touch,' JB said with a smile. Then he ended the call and sent Milo a text with Grosvenor's number, telling him the new plan.

He closed his eyes and listened to the sound of the prison around him. Everyone was locked away for the night but it was still noisy. Everything about prison life was noisy. Still, at least he had a cell to himself now, and he could relax a little knowing that Grosvenor would take care of Savage for him and hopefully the annoying little prick would be out of the country and out of his hair soon enough. Then once everything had settled down again, he could go back to getting on with his only remaining goal in life – bringing down Grace Carter and her entire family for good.

Chapter Two

J ake Conlon smiled as he watched his best friend, and the man who was a brother to him in every way, at work. He really was a ruthless bastard and his skill for making people talk was a thing of beauty to witness. Currently, he had his size-eleven boot pressed against the neck of some poor fucker who was their most recent lead in the hunt for Milo Savage.

'You fucking worked with him, you cunt,' Connor spat as he pressed the heel of his boot into the soft skin of the man's throat, making him gasp for breath. 'Now tell me where the fuck he is or you will be eating through a straw for the rest of your life.'

'I don't know. I haven't seen him for years,' the man croaked as he wheezed under the pressure on his windpipe. 'I swear.' Tears ran from his eyes and onto the concrete his face was squashed against, making him look like a Mr Potato Head that had melted in the sun.

Connor looked at Jake and shook his head. They both knew this was a dead end, just like every other lead they had chased in the past three weeks. Milo Savage seemed to have no friends left in the world. But if that was true, where the fuck was he?

'You think he's telling us the truth, Jake?' Connor asked as he applied a little more pressure to the man's neck, making his eyes bulge in their sockets. Jake wasn't against violence, in fact he quite enjoyed it, but over the past three weeks they'd managed to interrogate dozens of people while not killing any of them. That might not sound like much but it was a huge feat for Connor Carter, who had gone after Milo Savage with a determination that Jake hadn't seen in him for a while. Milo had threatened Connor's wife, Jazz, and he'd tried to have Connor framed for murder, and had almost succeeded. He was also responsible for Danny being locked up for murder too. There was no doubt that Milo Savage was the most wanted man alive, but racking up a massive body count while looking for him wasn't the smartest move and Jake was glad that his business partner agreed with him on this one.

However, it was becoming increasingly clear that Connor was reaching the end of his tether. If he didn't find Milo soon, then people were going to start dying because it was only so long that he could keep a lid on his epic temper.

Jake watched as the man on the floor struggled, gasping for air and turning a strange shade of purple as his features transformed under Connor's weight. He couldn't talk now even if he wanted to. But Jake and Connor knew he had nothing to say. Connor had spent half an hour torturing him before they'd got to this point. It was true he had once worked with Milo and Sol Shepherd and he'd been one of the drivers who had ferried the women they bought and sold to the various sex parties they were forced to attend, but he wasn't tough or loyal enough to have lasted this long without giving anything up.

'I don't think he knows anything, Con,' Jake said, but it was already too late. Connor lifted his other foot from the floor until almost his entire muscular six-foot frame was crushing the man's windpipe. He gave a final choking sound before blood ran from his nose and sputtered out of his mouth.

'Fuck, Con,' Jake said with a sigh.

'He was a fucking piece of shit,' Connor barked. 'You know what he used to do with those girls. Jazz told me he was a handsy fucker when he worked at the club too.' He took his foot off the man's neck and stepped back to admire his handiwork.

'Yeah, but now we've got to get someone to come clean him up off the floor,' Jake said with a shake of his head. Had he known what Jazz had told her incredibly possessive and overprotective husband beforehand, Jake would have been more prepared for the day to end this way. As it was, he was supposed to be meeting Danny for dinner in an hour. It wasn't just any dinner either. He was going to ask Danny something and he already felt nervous as fuck about it. He and Danny were pretty inseparable, and he loved the man so much, sometimes it felt like he couldn't breathe without him. He knew that Danny loved him too, but coming out was a recent development in Danny's life and Jake still sensed some hesitation in him at times, so he wasn't sure how his suggestion to officially live together was going to go down.

They practically lived together anyway, but Danny still had his house in Anfield, and he still referred to that place as his home rather than Jake's apartment on the waterfront. He also made a thing about going back there once a week to check on the place and 'get his stuff', like he was just having a sleepover at Jake's rather than living there.

'I'll sort it,' Connor said as he glanced at his watch. 'You get off.'

Jake looked at Connor and then back at the dead man on the floor. 'I can't leave you to it.'

'But aren't you popping the question tonight?' Connor asked, raising an eyebrow. He and Jake never kept any secrets from each other and Jake had told his stepbrother of his plans.

'I'm not asking him to fucking marry me,' Jake said, shaking his head.

'Might as well be. That's the next step,' Connor replied with a smile.

'Fuck! Can you imagine Danny agreeing to get married? He can barely hold my hand in fucking public without coming out in hives.'

Connor laughed as he walked over to Jake and put an

arm around his shoulder. 'Yeah, but he fucking loves you though, mate. Everyone can see that.'

'Yeah?' Jake smiled at him, unable to hide the happiness that made him feel.

'Yeah,' said Connor. 'So get going and I'll sort this.'

'It'll be quicker if we both do it. Let's just get it done, eh?' Jake replied.

'Sound. I'll go get the bleach from the car. Can you call Nudge and tell him to expect a deposit?'

Jake nodded his agreement as he took his phone from his jacket pocket. Nudge Richards was the best fence in Merseyside and beyond. He also owned a scrapyard and it was the perfect place to deal with the disposal of dead bodies. Nudge had been loyal to Jake's mum, Grace Carter, since before she'd even been a Carter, and he'd remained loyal to Jake and Connor after she stepped aside. Nudge was paid well for his services, but that was because his services were so prized. He could be counted on to ensure no trace remained of the dead man on the floor once Jake and Connor had dropped him off at his yard.

Jake dialled his number and waited for Nudge to answer. At least dealing with a dead body would take his mind off dinner with Danny.

Chapter Three

Danny Alexander looked at his watch as he waited for Jake. He was late. Not that it mattered all that much to Danny, because he knew he was out with Connor looking for Milo Savage, and Danny wanted that fucker found just as much as anyone. It was Savage's fault that Danny had spent two weeks in Walton prison for his own mother's murder. He felt a wave of guilt washing over him as he thought about Glenda. They'd had a difficult relationship, to say the least, and certainly in recent years she had done nothing but cause him and his sister, Stacey, aggravation, but she was still his mum. She'd suffered when she had been killed and he hated thinking of her crying out in pain for him.

'Can I get you anything else?' the dark-haired waitress asked with a smile.

'Not just now, thanks.'

'You been stood up?' she asked him.

'Not yet,' he laughed. She stood there, chewing on her lip in a way that he'd bet most men kind of liked. She was pretty. She had a great smile and an amazing figure too. He wondered if he should tell her that she was barking up the wrong tree.

'I can't believe anyone would stand you up,' she purred as she reached for his almost empty glass, her fingers brushing his hand as she did. 'Let me get you a refill on the house.'

'Aren't they free?' he asked. He was driving so he was only drinking Coke. Jake had asked him to choose the restaurant for dinner tonight and he had chosen a Beefeater pub, much to Jake's disgust. But it had always been Danny's favourite place to eat. He loved a good steak without anything fancy. He never got to go out anywhere to eat as a kid and maybe it was that which made the place feel like a treat to him. Besides, Jake's family owned a string of high-priced, fancy restaurants, and they could eat stuff like that any time they wanted.

'Well, yes,' she giggled. 'But I can get you an extra lemon wedge if you're nice to me.'

There was a time he would have jumped at the chance to take a girl like her back to his house for a night, and he did so frequently, rarely offering a second date – unless they gave amazing head, and then he might consider it. He didn't do relationships or feelings. But all that stopped when he met Jake Conlon.

Danny could hardly believe it himself – who would have thought he'd get the best head of his life from another man?

– and the most eligible bachelor in Liverpool at that. He smiled at the thought and made the waitress giggle louder, mistakenly thinking it was aimed at her.

He was about to tell her that he wasn't interested when he felt a warm hand sliding around his neck. The smell of Jake's distinctive aftershave made his heart race a little faster – not only because Jake's presence usually had that effect on him, but also because he was going to think he'd been flirting with the waitress. He was a jealous fucker sometimes, but Danny actually quite liked it – it made him feel wanted and like he belonged to someone else.

'Sorry I'm late,' Jake said as he turned Danny's head and kissed him. Not a peck on the cheek either, but a full-on tonguing.

Danny felt the heat creeping over his neck at Jake's blatant display of possessiveness and ownership. He hated public displays of affection, but he could do nothing but accept Jake's demanding embrace. When he finally let him up for air, Jake looked at their waitress, who stood staring at the two of them in shock. 'Can I get a bottle of Bud?' he asked before he took a seat opposite Danny.

'Y-yeah,' she stammered.

'And I will take that refill, thanks. But you can hold the extra lemon,' Danny said.

She nodded and walked away and Jake laughed softly.

'Did you have to do that?' Danny asked him, but with a grin on his face.

Jake shrugged. 'Do women flirt with you every single place you go?'

Danny stared at him. He couldn't tell whether Jake was annoyed or not, but he had a cocky grin on his face so he assumed not. 'I have to put up with women and men flirting with you everywhere we go, so...' Danny replied.

It was true that women often flirted with him, but people practically threw themselves at Jake. He looked just like a younger, hotter version of Tom Hardy. Only two nights earlier, one of the new bar staff from Jake's club, The Blue Rooms, had offered to give him a blow job in his office – right while Danny was standing there. Danny had punched him in the face for his trouble, so he supposed that he was a little possessive too.

'But I'm only interested in you. You know that, Dan.'

Danny swallowed. He did know that right now. But how long would it last? Surely it was only a matter of time before someone else caught Jake's attention. He was the whole fucking package. He'd never been into relationships in the past either, but he told Danny that he loved him. They spent every spare moment they had together and they never got bored of each other's company. They argued occasionally, but nothing that couldn't be resolved by sex or a film and a takeaway.

'Don't you?' Jake frowned at him.

'Yeah.'

'You don't sound all that convinced.'

'Well, fuck, Jake,' Danny sighed and ran a hand through his thick dark hair.

'What?' Jake leaned forward, placing his hands on the table.

'What if...' Danny swallowed. How did their conversation get so deep so fast?

'What if what, Dan?' Jake asked, the edge creeping into his voice.

'You get fed up of me or something?' he whispered.

'Fuck me, you're the most insecure person I've ever fucking met,' Jake said with a soft chuckle.

'Yeah, well, you try going out with someone that you know almost every other person you meet wants to be with too,' Danny retorted.

'I already do,' Jake reminded him. 'You're the complete package, Dan. Now I'm sorry your mum screwed you up and made you believe you were nothing, but you need to shake this not-feeling-good-enough shit. There is a reason that hot little waitress was flirting with you when I came in.'

Danny stared at him across the table.

'And there is a reason I stuck my tongue down your throat when I saw her doing it,' he went on.

'I thought that was just because you're a jealous arsehole,' Danny said with a grin, trying to lighten the mood.

'I am when it comes to you.' Jake winked at him. 'But I can't believe I offer to take you out for dinner and you make us come here,' he added as he looked around the pub.

'There is fuck-all wrong with this place,' Danny protested as the waitress came back with their drinks.

Danny was finishing the last bite of his steak when he looked up to see Jake staring at him.

'I'm starving,' he said apologetically as he wiped his mouth, wondering if he'd just made himself look like a complete glutton as he inhaled his dinner.

'I wanted to talk to you about something,' Jake replied as he placed his knife and fork carefully on the table.

Danny's stomach dropped as he wondered what was about to happen. The 'we need to talk' conversation was never a good one, was it? Or so he'd heard. He'd never actually had one before, preferring to ghost any previous conquests who might have got the idea he was looking for anything more than a quick hook-up, until they got fed up of badgering him. He looked closely at Jake. 'About what?'

'I want you to move in with me,' Jake replied.

Danny's steak dinner threatened to make a sudden reappearance. 'What?'

'You practically live at my place anyway. Why not make it permanent?'

'But it's your place, Jake, not mine,' Danny replied. His little house in Anfield might not be much compared to Jake's penthouse suite, and he could certainly afford to get himself a better place now, but he had worked hard to buy himself that house. It was the first place that had belonged only to him, and as much as Jake was right about him spending most of his time at Jake's place anyway, it wasn't the same as actually living with him.

'Then we'll buy somewhere else?' Jake replied with a shrug. 'Somewhere that belongs to both of us.'

Danny's fork clattered onto his plate as he dropped it in shock. This couldn't be real. This was way more than moving in together. 'Like we'll buy a place? Together? Me and you?'

'For fuck's sake, Dan. Yes!' Jake said with a shake of his head, wondering why this was such a big deal. As far as he was concerned life was far too short to not go after what you wanted – and what he wanted was the man sitting opposite him, who was staring at him like he'd just grown an extra head. 'I've been thinking about getting a place with a garden anyway, now that Isla is with me more.'

Isla was Jake's eight-year-old daughter with his ex-wife, Siobhan. He'd married her when he was nineteen and trying to convince the rest of the world he was straight. They had both made mistakes – she'd tricked him into marrying her and he had cheated on her with his best mate, Paul. They'd had an acrimonious end, to put it mildly, but they had been friends for a long time before they got together, and somehow they had managed to forgive each other and become friends again, and co-parents to their daughter. When she'd had a few glasses of wine, Siobhan would proudly declare that she was the only girl Jake would ever love and it always made him laugh because he supposed it was true.

'But it will be mine *and* yours?' Danny asked with a frown.

'I'm happy to put more money in – let's face it, I could do with putting it somewhere – but yes, it will be ours. Mine *and* yours.'

'I'll pay my full half,' Danny insisted.

Jake bit back a smile. Danny's fierce independence was one of the many things he admired about him. 'So you're up for it then?'

'I'm not selling my old place though. Not because I want to live in it, b-but...' Danny stammered.

'I know,' Jake assured him. Danny had brought himself and his little sister Stacey up. He'd never had much as a kid and Jake knew how much the first place he'd ever called a real home meant to him. 'Maybe you could rent it out to one of the lads?'

'Maybe.' The hint of a smile flickered over Danny's face.

'There's a house right by Connor's up for sale.'

'You been looking already?' Danny grinned at him.

'Maybe. And I might have booked us a viewing for tomorrow afternoon.'

'You're so fucking sure of yourself.'

'No.' Jake shook his head. 'I see what I want and I go after it, Dan.'

'And you want a huge detached house in Mossley Hill right by your best mate?'

'I want you,' Jake said, his tone low and demanding and sending a shiver of excitement up Danny's spine. 'I don't give a fuck where we live.'

Before Danny could reply, Jake's mobile started ringing on the table in front of them. Connor's name was flashing on the screen and Jake frowned as he picked it up. Connor had dropped him off less than an hour ago on his way to Nudge Richards' place.

'Jake, you need to get your arse down here. Now!'

'Why? What's going on?'

'He's dead, Jake.'

'I know. You crushed his fucking windpipe.'

'Not him, soft lad. Nudge.'

'Nah. I spoke to him two hours ago,' Jake snapped, thinking somehow Connor must be mistaken. Nudge loved a drink. Maybe he'd just passed out.

'Someone slit his fucking throat and left him to bleed out, Jake. He's as dead as the cunt I brought in here half an hour ago.'

'Fuck!' Jake ran a hand over his face as his heart started to race. Who the fuck would want to kill Nudge? And who the hell had got to him between when Jake last spoke to him and Connor's arrival there half an hour ago? 'Have you called anyone else yet?'

'No. I only just found him. Get your arse down here so I can figure what the fuck to do with two fucking dead bodies, mate.'

'We're on our way.'

Chapter Four

Danny floored the accelerator as he raced down the M57 toward Nudge's scrapyard in the south of the city. He'd called his business partner, and Jake's uncle, Luke, to meet them there too. A situation of this magnitude would require all of them to sort it out.

'Who would do that to Nudge?' Danny asked as Jake chewed his thumbnail.

'I don't know,' he mumbled.

'You think it was anything to do with us? With Milo Savage, maybe?'

Jake shook his head. 'Nudge worked with anyone and everyone. He was a huge gambler too. He reined it in in recent years, but he was a sucker for the horses.'

'But if he'd had a debt he couldn't pay, we'd have known about it.'

'Hmm.' Jake stared out of the window as it started to rain. 'He loved his women too.'

'Maybe he fucked with the wrong one?' Danny offered.

'Or just fucked the wrong one? We'll know more once we get there, so put your fucking foot down, Dan.'

'I'm doing eighty, Jake,' Danny said with a roll of his eyes.

'You're driving a fucking Maserati, mate. This thing does eighty in fourth gear.'

'Yeah, but the last thing we need right now is to get pulled by the bizzies, isn't it?'

'Just get us where we need to be, Dan,' Jake snapped as he turned back to the window. He knew he shouldn't take his frustration out on Danny, but Nudge being killed had rattled him. Not only because they had made it known that the man was untouchable, but also because he'd lost count of the number of bodies they'd disposed of there. Fuck! He had no idea if Nudge had any family or who the hell would take over the place now that he was gone. But besides that, the yard was now a murder scene, and once the bizzies started crawling all over the place, how soon before they found a stray body part or the DNA of someone on the missing list and started asking questions?

'Fuck!' Jake muttered and Danny squeezed his thigh reassuringly.

'We'll sort everything. It will be fine.'

'Yeah,' Jake agreed but he didn't share Danny's optimism.

When the car pulled up outside Nudge's scrapyard fifteen minutes later, Connor and Luke were waiting by the huge steel gates. Danny drove through them and rolled the car to a stop while Luke closed the gates behind them. Connor walked straight to the car as Jake and Danny climbed out.

'Where is he?' Jake asked, a shudder running down his spine as he looked around the yard. It was dark and he found the place creepy enough in the daylight.

'They left the poor old fucker in a beat-up Merc round the back,' Connor said with a shake of his head.

'And nobody was here when you arrived?' Jake quizzed him.

'No. At least not that I saw. He'd left the gates unlocked and when I went to his Portakabin he wasn't there. I assumed he'd gone for a shit, or nipped to the bookies and got distracted. You know how he is.'

'How he was,' Jake reminded him and Connor shuddered.

'His throat was cut?' Danny asked as he walked around the car and stood beside Jake.

'Yep,' Connor replied. 'I didn't pull him out of the car yet. We're gonna have to decide what to do with him.'

'I know,' Jake said with a sigh. 'There's no way we can have this place becoming a murder scene.'

'Too fucking right,' Connor murmured.

'So what do we do?' Danny asked as he looked between his two employers. Luke joined them and he too stood waiting for some direction.

'We need to think. I mean, this is Nudge we're talking about. We can't just bury him in a ditch somewhere,' Jake said.

'Yeah. Then there's this place,' Luke added. 'I mean, who the fuck does it go to with Nudge gone? He's got no family, right?'

'Nope,' said Connor.

They were distracted by headlights and the beeping of a car.

'Who the fuck's that?' Jake hissed as he turned his head towards the noise.

'That'll be Jazz. John brought her,' Connor replied as he started to make his way back to the gate. 'They got here quicker than I expected.'

'You called Jazz?' Jake asked his best mate as he fell into step beside him. Not that he didn't value her opinion, but Connor had her practically under lock and key while Milo Savage was still at large.

'I made sure John picked her up,' Connor replied, understanding Jake's reservations without him having to say them aloud. John Brennan was their most trusted employee and he was also one of the few people Connor would trust with his wife's safety. John was skilled and ruthless and he was practically family too.

'And what choice did I have?' Connor went on. 'She's the head of Cartel Securities, Jake. Besides, she can think things through in a way none of us can, mate. She's like your mum that way, and I didn't want to call her.'

'No. Of course not. Not yet,' Jake agreed. His mum had always had a soft spot for Nudge. She had saved his life years earlier and he had remained steadfastly loyal to her ever since. She was going to be devastated when she found out, especially given the circumstances of his demise. Jake knew he was going to have to work hard to convince her not to get on the first plane back home and start a war to find Nudge's killer. Maybe if he spoke to his stepdad, Michael, first, he'd be able to help talk some sense into her.

Connor and Jake swung open the gates and John pulled his X5 into the yard. 'We expecting anyone else?' Jake asked as they closed the heavy steel gates again.

'No. Anyone else comes through these tonight, we should probably just shoot them,' Connor laughed.

'You pretend you're joking but it's true, Con. We've got two fucking dead bodies to deal with now,' Jake said.

'Fuck!' Connor mumbled. 'I should have been in bed with my missus by now instead of dealing with this shit. And I know I ruined your big night, mate. I'm sorry I lost it.'

'Don't be. If you hadn't had to come here to deal with that prick, you wouldn't have found Nudge. Then fuck knows who would have. There would have been bizzies crawling all over the place by tomorrow night. You did us a favour, mate.'

As soon as John's car came to a stop, Connor walked to it and opened the passenger door for his wife while John jumped out of the driver's side. Taking her hand, Connor helped her climb out and then he gave her a brief kiss before they both walked toward the rest of the group. All six of them stood in the middle of the scrap yard in the fading light, looking at each other and waiting for the answers to their current problem.

Luckily for all of them, Jasmine Carter had them.

Chapter Five

Jasmine sat down on one of the chairs in Nudge's office as Connor, Jake, Luke, Danny and John all found themselves somewhere to sit or stand.

'So tell us exactly what happened,' she said to Connor.

'I got here just after eight o'clock. The gates were open, but then Jake had asked Nudge to open up for us, so...'

'And what time did you speak to him?' Jazz asked, turning her attention to Jake now.

'Maybe seven, was it?' Jake looked at Connor, who nodded.

'And was he already here when you called him?' Jazz asked.

'Yeah, but he practically lives here. He's set himself up a bed and everything in that new Portakabin he got.'

'True,' Jazz replied thoughtfully. 'So anyone looking for him would automatically come here.' She said that last part to herself.

'He wasn't in there or in here when I got here, so I assumed he'd be back in a few minutes,' Connor added. 'I locked the gates and got on with what I needed to do.'

'And you saw nothing suspicious, mate?' Luke asked him.

'No. The place was deserted. At least it looked that way, or I wouldn't have started carving up a dead body. But then I wasn't looking for anyone, was I?'

'So how did you come to find him?' Jazz asked.

'I needed the key to the lockup where we keep the good tools. I'd kind of done all I could with the axe,' Connor replied matter of factly, as though chopping up a dead body was all in a day's work. 'So I went looking for Nudge. I found him sitting in a car around the back. I thought he'd just fallen asleep at first. I even called him a lazy old cunt. Fuck! If I'd have got here even a few minutes earlier I might have caught the fuckers...' Connor trailed off, shaking his head.

'Then whoever killed Nudge might have hurt you too,' Jazz said.

'You think this was anything to do with Milo?' Jake asked with a scowl.

'Why would he go after Nudge though?' Jazz replied. 'It doesn't serve any purpose to him.'

'I agree with Jazz,' Connor replied. 'There is no reason for Milo to go after him.'

'You think it was anything to do with us at all?' Danny asked and they all looked at each other and then at John Brennan, who had known Nudge longer than any of them.

'Who the fuck knows?' John replied with a shake of his head. 'Nudge knew everyone worth knowing. He was discreet and that's why people would come to him. Maybe he had information that someone else wanted. Maybe he pissed off the wrong person. Maybe he screwed the wrong wife? It could be fucking anything. I spoke to him last week and he never mentioned he was having any trouble with anyone. He'd just had a win on the horses and was as happy as a pig in shit.'

'What the fuck do we do then?' Jake asked.

'We can't let the police find his body here,' Jazz answered. 'As painful as this sounds, nobody but us is really going to miss Nudge. The type of people he worked with aren't the kind to report his sudden disappearance to the police. As far as we know, he retired and moved to the Costa Del Sol to live out his final years in the sunshine.'

'He always did say he'd like to do that. Poor fucker,' John said with a sigh.

'And what about this place, Jazz?' asked Jake. 'Who takes control of this place when Nudge retires? Because I'm pretty sure the bizzies and the tax man will be all over it if Nudge suddenly gifts his business to one of us, which, face it, is what needs to happen because we cannot risk anyone outside of our family getting their hands on this yard.'

Jazz leaned back in her chair and smiled. Grace Carter was a genius. 'This place hasn't belonged to Nudge for a long time,' she said slowly, making everyone else in the room stare at her in confusion.

'What?' Jake snapped.

'It's been owned by Sumner Enterprises for the last five years.'

'Sumner Enterprises?' Jake replied, his frown deepening. 'That's…'

'… your mum's maiden name and a subsidiary of Cartel Securities,' Luke finished for him.

'Yeah.' Jake nodded. 'How the fuck did we not know that?'

'Well, your mum quietly bought the place years ago and allowed Nudge to remain in control, but all of the paperwork and the accounts are in our company name,' Jazz said proudly. She had only discovered this fact herself after she had taken over as CEO of Cartel Securities. The company had numerous subsidiaries and they had businesses all over the place that they had little direct involvement in. Grace Carter was a shrewd businesswoman and she had built her family's empire quietly and diligently without many people even noticing. 'I can manage the books for the place, but we need someone in here to manage the day-to-day. Someone we can trust, who won't ask questions.'

'The scrappy is just a cover for all of the other stuff Nudge was involved in,' said Luke. 'It doesn't really do that much scrap metal business. Me and Danny can base ourselves here for a few weeks while we find the right man for the job.'

'Or woman?' Jazz added.

'Or woman,' Luke agreed with a smile.

'Fuck, your mum is a dark horse, Jake,' Connor said with a shake of his head.

'You really think she'd have let you lot do what we do here without knowing this place would never fall into the wrong hands?' John said with a chuckle.

'You knew about this, big fella?' Connor asked him with a frown.

'I didn't know the detail, but I know her well enough to know she wouldn't let her husband and sons carve up and hide bodies in a yard that she didn't have full control of.'

'So we don't have to worry on that score then,' Jake said with a sigh of relief.

'And that means I can finish up sorting out the body I brought here earlier then?' Connor asked.

Jazz looked at her husband and then at John, who rolled his eyes before saying, 'I'll take care of that for you, boss.'

'Nice one, John,' Connor replied gratefully.

'You need any help, mate?' Luke offered.

'Yeah, if you're free?'

'Stacey is working, and I promised to pick her up later, so...' Luke replied with a shrug. He had been going out with Danny's younger sister for a while, although they'd had a rough patch recently when Stacey and Danny found out Luke had lied to them about their mum coming back to look for them years earlier. But they were working through it and Luke was determined to make his girlfriend forgive him. He was made up to see his best mate, Danny, happy and loved up with Jake, and he wanted the same for himself. He'd liked Stacey for a long time, but they'd both tried to fight their attraction to each other because of how Danny might react to his best mate being with his little sister. Danny had ended up taking the news surprisingly well, but then he had been sneaking around with Jake at the time.

'And what do we do with poor old Nudge then?' Jake asked as he looked around the room.

'Clean and crush the car. Then we'll bury him somewhere no one will ever find him,' Connor replied before turning to his wife. 'Looks like I won't be home early after all, babe. Sorry.'

Jazz shook her head. 'Don't worry. This is more important.' She was well aware that her husband was the most experienced and skilled amongst them at disposing of bodies, and they needed all this dealt with as quickly and cleanly as possible.

'Me and you can sort Nudge then, Jake. We'll bury him properly somewhere. Dan, can you take Jazz home for me?'

'I can drive myself home, Connor—' Jazz said but he interrupted her mid-sentence.

'While that cunt Milo is still out there, you're going nowhere on your own, babe. I know you can handle yourself, but he is a sick fucker and he's obsessed with you. Who knows what the fuck he'll do next. And we don't know for certain he wasn't behind this tonight.'

'I can drive you home, Jazz. It's not a problem,' Danny assured her.

'Thanks,' she said with a soft sigh. Connor reached for

her hand and laced his fingers through hers. 'I can't have anything happening to you,' he said to her.

'I know,' she whispered.

'Who's gonna tell Grace about Nudge?' John asked, reminding them of the other huge problem they were facing. Grace Carter was not going to take the news of one of her oldest friends' demise very well.

'I'll tell her,' Jake replied. 'But not tonight. Nobody but us knows about him, so just give me a day or two to figure out what I'm going to say to her, okay?'

'And the killer,' Danny added. 'He knows too.'

'I doubt he's gonna go telling people he offed Nudge Richards though, is he, Dan?' Jake replied with a frown.

'I'm just saying,' Danny said with a shrug.

'Are we going to sort this mess out then? We can talk through all the other shit tomorrow,' Connor said as he stood up.

'Yeah, let's get a move on,' Jake agreed.

'You ready to go now, Jazz?' Danny asked her.

'You sure you don't need me for anything else?' she asked as she pushed herself up from her chair, directing her question to Jake and Connor.

'No, babe. You get off. Danny will wait with you till I get home. I won't be too late,' Connor replied as he slid an arm around her waist and kissed her cheek.

'Okay. Be careful, all of you,' she replied before she followed Danny out of Nudge's office.

Jazz settled back against the warm leather seat of Danny's car. Her mind raced with questions. Who had killed poor Nudge? How was Grace going to take the news? Would she cut her trip to Spain short and come home to deal with things herself? Or would she trust that Jazz and the boys could handle it without her?

Jazz hoped for the latter. She missed Grace and Michael, and their youngest children Belle and Oscar, but Grace's had been big shoes to fill, and it was only now that Jazz was starting to feel worthy of them. She was finally getting to grips with all aspects of the business and she'd even identified some new, legitimate ventures for Cartel Securities to invest in. She knew how much Grace and Michael wanted their whole organisation to be legit one day, and although she was fully aware of what Connor did and had no qualms about the nature of his business, she did hope that one day they could leave it all behind them and focus on the legal, and less dangerous, side of life.

They had their young son to think of now, and she hoped to have more children in a few years. She would sleep better at night knowing that she and her husband didn't have any number of unknown enemies waiting to steal their crown. Not to mention the constant worry of the police pinning something on them. Cartel Securities and their subsidiary companies certainly had enough income to keep them all busy, and comfortable, but Jazz knew better than most how difficult it was to walk away from the kind of life she and her family led.

The fact that she was even contemplating a different

future was a shock to her. She'd never thought about it before, but she supposed her recent brush with her ex-husband's right-hand man Milo Savage had affected her more than she would care to admit. She looked out of the window and sighed softly.

'You okay, Jazz?' Danny asked her, his voice full of concern.

She turned to face him. She loved Danny. He was the perfect partner for Jake Conlon. He kept him grounded and in line in a way that very few people were able to. He was the whole package too – handsome, loyal and smart, and yet incredibly humble too. In that last respect, he was the complete opposite of Jake, who was cocky and self-assured.

'I'm worried, Danny. I mean, who would kill Nudge like that? And why?'

'I haven't got the foggiest,' he replied with a shrug. 'I wish I did.'

'It unnerves me when I don't have any answers at all. I mean, I don't even know where to start. He never had any real enemies, did he? I mean, none that would do something like that? So, what if it's about something much bigger?'

'Or maybe he did just piss off the wrong person? Maybe some fella found out he was banging his missus and lost it?'

'To slit his throat like that and leave him in a car to find? That doesn't seem like an impulsive crime of passion to me,' she replied with a shake of her head. 'It feels too professional.'

'We'll get some sleep and then we'll find some answers. Someone will know something,' Danny offered.

'Yeah, but we go rattling too many cages and then people will start wondering why we're so concerned about a man who we're going to tell everyone has retired to the Costa Del Sol.'

'Fuck, yeah,' Danny sighed.

'And we can't risk anyone finding out he's been murdered, or the police will pick over that yard with a fine-tooth comb, and who knows what they'll find.'

'Yeah.' Danny rubbed a hand over his jaw. 'Which makes me think we need to have a clear-out ourselves once the dust has settled. Who knows what might happen in the future, Jazz? If there is any evidence of the stuff we've done over the years in that place, then we need to get rid of it.'

'I couldn't agree more,' she said. 'Anyway, tell me, how was your dinner tonight?'

Danny arched an eyebrow at her. 'We had a steak in a pub, Jazz. Not much to tell.'

She narrowed her eyes at him. 'Is that all?'

'Why? Do you know something I don't?'

She stared at him. Hadn't Jake asked him to move in? Connor had told her that he was planning to, but maybe he hadn't? She hoped she hadn't ruined the surprise. However, the slight smirk on Danny's face now told her that she hadn't.

'Well, I don't know what you know, so…' she replied.

'Is nothing ever a secret in your family?' He laughed softly. 'I mean, what if I'd said no?'

Jazz laughed too. 'Connor and Jake tell each other everything, Danny. You need to get used to that. So you didn't say no then? You're moving in with him?'

'We're going to look at a place together,' Danny replied.

'The house by us?' she squealed. It would be so nice to have Jake and Danny close by.

'Fuck, he really does tell him everything. Yes, we're looking at it tomorrow.'

'Imagine us being neighbours,' she said with a huge smile on her face.

'Yeah,' Danny replied, keeping his eyes fixed firmly on the road and not returning her smile.

'Don't you want to be our neighbours then?' Jazz teased him, giving him a nudge on the arm. 'It's okay. I get it if you want your own private little love nest somewhere.'

'It's not that, Jazz,' Danny said with a sigh.

She sat a little straighter in her seat and frowned at him. 'What's wrong? Are you having second thoughts?'

She saw his Adam's apple bob as he swallowed and a feeling of dread settled over her. If he broke Jake's heart...

'What if I buy a house with him and then he changes his mind? What would I do then?' He turned to her and the self-doubt that was written all over his face made her want to hug him.

'Oh, Dan,' she placed her hand on his arm and squeezed instead. 'Jake adores you. Can't you see that?'

'I know he loves me, Jazz. For now at least,' he said as he turned back to the road.

'You think that kind of love is only temporary?' She laughed softly.

'What if it is, though? What if he meets someone else?'

'He doesn't even see anyone else when you're in the room, Danny. Do you not think Jake has insecurities too? But you have to just grab life by the balls and take a chance at everything – especially love.'

'Jake Conlon doesn't know the meaning of the word insecurity,' Danny said with a light laugh.

'You think he's not terrified of losing you too?' Jazz said softly.

Danny turned to her again, looking puzzled.

'He already lost the only other man he loved. You didn't even know you were bisexual until a few months ago, and, let's face it, you were just as much of a player as he was. You think he doesn't worry about you changing your mind too?'

'I never thought of it like that,' Danny admitted. 'He's such a cocky bastard.'

'Well, you're right there.' Jazz laughed again. 'But he loves you, idiot.'

'Thanks, Jazz,' Danny replied as he suddenly realised that Jake had just as much reason to doubt their relationship as he did, but despite that he was all in. Maybe it was time for Danny to be all in too.

Chapter Six

Jake wiped the beads of sweat and dirt from his brow as he straightened up. He stared at the body of Nudge Richards. They had wrapped him in clear tarpaulin and his features were barely visible now. In a few minutes, he'd be rolled into the five-foot hole he and Connor had just finished digging and no one would ever see him again – at least that was the plan. Nudge had been a loyal soldier, and a friend to his mum. He deserved a proper burial, but they couldn't afford to give him one. Jake consoled himself with the fact that Nudge, of all people, would understand what they were doing. The old fucker might haunt them for the rest of their lives for it, but he would understand.

'You ready?' Connor grunted as he lifted one half of the dead body. He was much more used to these situations than Jake was. He preferred to keep his hands as clean as possible these days, but he reminded himself that they hadn't actually killed this one, they were just disposing of his body.

'Yep,' Jake replied as he bent down and picked up the feet and together they hoisted Nudge's huge corpse into the hole in the middle of the woods. He fell to the bottom with a dull thud and the two men stood beside his final resting place in silence.

'You think we should say anything?' Jake finally whispered.

'Maybe,' Connor replied with a shrug. 'I mean I wouldn't usually, but…'

'We don't usually bury our mates?' Jake finished for him. 'At least not like this.'

'Nope,' Connor agreed with a sigh. 'You do it then.'

Jake stared at the body in the ground. 'Rest in peace, Nudge. At least it actually is peaceful round here, mate,' he said as he looked around in the darkness. The only light came from the almost full moon and their large torch on the ground.

'Save us a good spot in hell, lad,' Connor added.

'I'm not going to hell,' Jake said with a frown as he stared at his stepbrother.

'Yes, you fucking are,' Connor laughed softly.

'Nah. I'm gonna repent all my sins on my deathbed, me.' Jake laughed too.

'You reckon Nudge got much time to repent?' Connor asked as he looked down at the outline of the body in the hole again.

'I doubt it, mate. Looked like it was quick at least,' Jake

replied. They'd both noticed that Nudge had no injuries other than the fatal one across his throat.

'Who the fuck would want to kill you, Nudge?' Connor asked quietly, still staring into the hole.

'We'll figure it out,' Jake assured him.

'Yeah. Now let's get this filled in and covered up so I can get home to my wife.'

The two of them hurriedly shovelled the earth back into the hole, covering up their dead associate inch by inch until the hole was full again. Then they scattered around the displaced earth and covered the grave with leaves, moss and twigs until they were satisfied it no longer looked like one.

'You think you could remember where he is? You know, if my mum asks?' Jake said.

'The general vicinity, yeah.'

'Let's get going then, eh?'

'Hmm,' Connor mumbled as he picked up the torch from the ground while Jake held onto the shovels. Then the two of them made their way through the trees and back to the clearing where they'd left the old Land Rover, leaving Nudge Richards alone in the cold, dark earth.

'I never asked how your dinner went,' Connor said as they walked back to the car.

'He said yes.' Jake laughed softly. The night's drama had almost made him forget about the earlier part of the evening when he'd asked Danny to move in with him. 'We're seeing that place by you tomorrow.'

'Nice,' said Connor approvingly.

'I hope he likes it, Con. I need a place with a garden for Isla now that she's getting older.'

'Yeah. Kids are gonna need space.'

'Kids?' Jake laughed loudly. 'I think "kid" is going to have to be my limit.'

'Why?'

'Well, me and Danny are kind of missing some vital pieces of equipment, mate.'

'I know that, soft shite. But you could adopt. Or get a surrogate. Or maybe even Siobhan would have another kid with you. She hasn't met anyone else yet, right?'

'I'm not sure that's the best idea,' Jake said with a laugh. 'I know we get on, mate, but I doubt she'd have another kid with me.'

'Danny then?' Connor suggested. 'I mean, he's still into women so they wouldn't even have to do the turkey baster thing, would they?' He laughed loudly, the sound echoing around the quiet woods.

'Fuck off, knobhead.' Jake gave him a nudge in the ribs but he laughed too. It was needed – the necessary break to separate what they had just done from the men they wanted to be when they went home to the people they loved.

Chapter Seven

J ohn climbed out of his car and walked up the path of his house. The light in the living room was on so he knew Leigh had waited up for him. No doubt she'd be reading the latest crime novel, as if she didn't get enough of the real thing in her day job. It had surprised nobody more than John himself when he had fallen for DI Leigh Moss. Of course he had known her way back in the day, when she'd been a stripper and not a copper, but still she was now one of Merseyside Police's most experienced and respected inspectors.

They'd had their fair share of ups and downs – one so bad it had ended their relationship completely. But they had been back together for a few weeks now, and had picked up exactly where they had left off. Both of them realised that life was too short not to spend it with the people who made you happy. And she did make him happy, and he knew that he did the same for her.

They had a rule that they never discussed each other's jobs, but they both knew that the roles they played in their very opposite worlds were a conflict of interest that they would have to resolve sooner rather than later. John had walked away from his former life once before for Leigh, only to have her dump him a few days later. He was prepared to do it for a second time if he had to, but he wanted some assurances from her first. Maybe even a ring on her finger? They'd have to run off and do it on their own if they ever did get married, obviously. He smiled to himself as he thought about a wedding reception if they didn't – with Merseyside Police on one side and the most notorious criminals in the city on the other.

He couldn't walk away right now anyway, not with Milo Savage still at large and Jazz in danger. Not to mention that what had happened to Nudge had thrown them all into disarray. Who the hell knew what that was about and whether it was something bigger?

He'd showered and changed at Luke's place after disposing of the dead body. Connor had been at his wits' end looking for Milo Savage over the past few weeks and John was surprised that there hadn't been more dead bodies piling up before now. Certainly the Connor of old would have handled things that way, but he really did seem to be maturing. Both he and Jake were turning into the kind of leaders that their parents had been and John, for one, couldn't be happier. It made his life a whole lot easier when the people at the top had everything in control. And of course, he couldn't discount Jazz's impact on the two of them. She was shrewd and calculating and ruthless when she needed to be, but she had a lot of compassion too. Grace had chosen the right woman to take over her helm.

The front door opened as John was about to put his key in the lock and Leigh stood on his doorstep with her arms folded across her chest. 'You were supposed to be home hours ago.'

'I told you I was going to be late, babe,' he said, stepping inside and leaning down to give her a soft kiss on the cheek.

'Do I want to know where you've been?' she asked, arching an eyebrow at him.

'Nope.' He closed the door behind him.

'Are you okay?' she asked, her tone softer as she placed a hand on his cheek.

'I'm fine. I'm sorry I'm late. Did you cook?' he asked, detecting the smell of curry. Leigh rarely cooked and she wasn't very good at it and suddenly John felt guilty for her wasted efforts.

'I poured a jar of sauce over some chicken. No big deal,' she said with a shrug, but he knew better. Cooking for him was a big thing for her. She'd been on her own and self-sufficient for most of her life. She didn't know how to do the whole caring-for-other-people thing, but the fact she was trying with him made him smile. He, on the other hand, loved to cook for her.

He slid his arms around her waist and pulled her closer. He wasn't in the mood for food, but he needed something to make him forget about the dead body he'd carved into pieces. 'I'll make it up to you. Promise,' he said with a grin.

'You'd better.' She grinned back.

'How was your day?'

Leigh rolled her eyes. 'Same old,' she said with a sigh. She headed up Merseyside Police force's special Phoenix team for dealing with rape and sexual assaults and John knew that her work took its toll on her. She wanted to give every victim a Rolls Royce service, but the truth was that she didn't have the resources or the manpower to do that and too many vulnerable women, and men, fell through the cracks. Bureaucracy and red tape often tied her hands and sometimes she envied John's world of acting without fear of the consequences.

At least the King brothers had finally been taken off the streets of Liverpool. Jerrod King was currently on remand, awaiting trial for the brutal murder of Danny's mother, Glenda, and his younger brother, Devlin, was supposedly on the run. Leigh wasn't naïve enough to think this was true. After the King brothers had murdered Danny's mother and tried to frame him for her murder, there was no way that he would be allowed to live. The fact that she'd not heard any whispers of Jake, Connor or even John looking for Devlin told her all she needed to know. Devlin King was dead, she was sure of it. And despite her general faith and belief in the criminal justice system, she couldn't bring herself to feel anything but glad that he was no longer terrorising the streets of Liverpool.

'Anything you want to talk about, Detective?' he asked.

She laughed softly at his gentle teasing before shaking her head. 'I'm tired.'

'Then let me take you to bed.' He laughed too as he hoisted her over his shoulder and made his way to the stairs.

Chapter Eight

DI Kevin Grosvenor was falling asleep when his phone started ringing on the bedside table. He groaned inwardly. He was the DI of the Major Incident Team, so being woken in the night wasn't an entirely unusual occurrence, unfortunately.

'Answer it, Kev,' his wife, Alison, groaned.

'Sorry, love,' he whispered. Glancing at the screen, he didn't recognise the number flashing on it. It wasn't the station or one of his colleagues. Muting the ring tone, he climbed out of bed and hurried from the bedroom before he answered.

'Hello?' he whispered as he made his way down the hallway to the stairs.

'Grosvenor?' the unfamiliar voice replied.

'Yeah.'

'A friend of mine said you could help me get out of the country.'

Kevin groaned inwardly as he started to make his way down the stairs. This was the call he'd been dreading and there was no getting back to sleep for him now. His heart started pounding as he wondered how the hell he was going to pull this off. He might mix with the worst kind of criminals that Liverpool had to offer, but he didn't know any of them personally. Certainly not well enough to ask them to get him a fake passport sorted. It was kind of his job not to know them that way.

'He asked me to help you, yeah,' Kevin said with a heavy sigh.

'Well, how quickly can you do it?' the voice snarled.

'I don't know. It will take some time. Maybe a few weeks.'

'A few weeks?' the man shouted. 'I haven't got a few weeks, Grosvenor! I'm a sitting fucking duck here.'

'Okay, calm the fuck down,' Kevin hissed. 'I can't just pull fake passports out of my arsehole.'

'Then you'd better get a new fucking arsehole, you cunt,' the other man hissed. 'Because I told Barrow I needed out by the end of the week, and if he can't deliver…'

'Then what?' Kevin swallowed. He didn't know who the hell this guy was or what he was capable of, but he did know that he needed to keep Barrow sweet and that meant trying to pacify the man on the other end of the phone.

'Then I'll deal with Barrow, and I'll come for you. I'll call you tomorrow and you'd better have some good news for me.'

Then the line went dead. Kevin placed his phone on the

table and put his head in his hands. Barrow had asked him for plenty of favours over the years. Mostly it was looking the other way or something to do with the job, and while he'd never been comfortable with any of the things he'd done, it had got easier over the years to stop listening to his conscience. But more importantly, they were things that were in his gift to do. This recent favour was completely out of his comfort zone and his area of expertise. What the fuck was he going to do?

He looked around the kitchen, as though that might offer him an answer to his prayers. This was his life. The pictures on the fridge that his kids had drawn in school. The flowers on the windowsill that he'd bought Alison last week for her birthday. The dozen different varieties of cereal on the countertop because that was what his teenagers seemed to live on these days. He'd worked hard to get where he was today. A nice four-bed semi in Allerton with a large garden and two decent cars on the drive. His four kids never went without anything. He was a good dad. A good husband. A good copper ninety-nine per cent of the time. He couldn't lose all of this because of one stupid mistake he made years ago. Kevin's heart sank as he realised he only had two options. He either had to sort out the passport and hope that Barrow kept his word about not asking for any more favours, which he knew was unlikely, or he had to remove the threat of Barrow for good. Neither of those options appealed to him, and he hated to admit that although he preferred the latter, he had absolutely no idea how he would go about it.

Kevin sat up for hours after his phone call. Going through scenarios in his head. Going over old cases where he might have met someone who could help him now. When he kept drawing a blank, he made himself a mug of coffee and picked up his phone. If John Barrow was going to land him in the shit, the least he could do was try and help him out a little.

'What?' Barrow answered the call after a few rings.

'I need your help with this passport issue, John,' Kevin admitted. 'I don't even know where to start.'

'I thought you were supposed to be one of Merseyside's shining lights, Grosvenor?' he sneered.

'Yeah, well, getting false passports isn't really in the job description,' Kevin snapped. He was tired and irritable and he wanted this whole fucking nightmare over with.

'A fence, Kevin,' Barrow replied dismissively, as though this was the most obvious solution in the world. 'You need a fence.'

'Right, okay,' he replied. Of course he did.

'Goodnight.'

'Hang on. Who even is this fella I'm doing this for? I can't get him a passport if I don't know anything about him.'

'Well, you don't need his name, do you? He wants a false one, obviously,' JB sneered again and Kevin put his fist in his mouth and bit down before he told Barrow what he really thought of him. The fact that the man was still an arrogant prick while sitting in a cell in Strangeways was laughable really.

'I still want it,' he finally said. 'And I need to know his age. I need a photo too.'

'He'll send you a photo when you've found someone to do it.'

'And his name?'

'Milo Savage. Look him up,' Barrow replied before the line went dead.

Kevin put his phone back on the table. That was twice he's been hung up on tonight – and by men who needed something from him. Arrogant pricks. Milo Savage? It didn't ring a bell, but he would be looking him up. There was no doubt about that.

Kevin drained his coffee and then looked down at the dark stain it had left on the mug. That was when it hit him. He did know a fence. Of course he did. The best fence in the North-West, by all accounts. Mervin Richards, although nobody ever referred to him by his given name and instead he was commonly known by his nickname, Nudge, even amongst the police. It was a nickname given to him decades earlier following an incident where he'd almost lost an eye, but now had a permanent disfigurement that made him appear like he was winking. *Nudge, nudge, wink wink.* Over the years, he had simply become known as Nudge.

Maybe tomorrow he would pay old Nudge a visit.

Chapter Nine

The sound of his mobile phone vibrating incessantly roused Jake from his sleep. He blinked at the clock on his nightstand. It was 9 a.m. but he hadn't got to bed until after four.

'Tell them to piss off,' Danny groaned beside him.

Jake picked up the phone and saw his ex-wife Siobhan's name flashing on the screen. Frowning, he answered the call.

'Hiya. Everything okay?'

'No,' Siobhan replied with a sigh. 'I just had a call from the wine bar. There was a break-in last night.'

'At Carters?' Jake snapped. Siobhan was the manager of his mum and Michael's wine bar in Lytham, although she did most of it remotely these days since returning to live in Liverpool.

'Yeah. They didn't get much, a few bottles of spirits, but

they made a right mess of the place. I need to go and survey the damage and show my face, but I don't want to take Isla with me. Can she stay with you and Danny for the day?'

'Course she can. We have to go somewhere this morning for half an hour, but I'll drop her with Connor and Jazz.' He didn't want Isla at the house-viewing because he didn't want his ex-wife knowing he was buying a place with his new boyfriend until it was definite. Not that he thought she'd give him grief – she had accepted him and Danny pretty well – but he knew it would bring up some old painful memories for her and it was a delicate conversation to have. He didn't want their daughter dropping him in it before he'd had a chance to tell her properly. They'd once had a house in Mossley Hill themselves – when he'd been pretending he was straight and happily married.

'Perfect. Can I drop her off in about half an hour?' she asked.

'Yeah.' Jake sat up in bed. 'I'll see you in a bit.'

He ended the call and nudged Danny awake. 'We've got Isla for the day,' he said as he climbed out of bed.

Danny sat up and rubbed the sleep from his eyes. 'Okay. We can take her to that new soft play place. They've got those huge inflatables.'

Jake smiled at him. He couldn't love Danny any more if he tried. 'You're just a big fucking kid, aren't ya?'

Danny shrugged. 'Who doesn't love a giant inflatable slide?'

Jake laughed as he walked to the en-suite. Danny adored

Isla and the feeling was mutual. She had been completely unfazed when Jake had told her that Danny was his boyfriend, but then he supposed that little kids didn't really see the world the same way adults did.

'You can mind our table while me and Isla have fun,' Danny shouted after him.

'Fine by me,' Jake shouted back. Then he turned on the shower and stepped beneath the scalding-hot water. While it was true they had some headaches to deal with, not least him telling his mum about Nudge's murder, Jake couldn't help smiling. He couldn't remember a time in his life when he'd been so happy. He really did have it all, and he would be fucked if he would let anyone take it away from him.

Jake watched Danny with his daughter, and his seven-month-old nephew Paul, in Connor and Jazz's garden and smiled. He hadn't always been the best dad to Isla, and after Connor's twin, Paul, was murdered, he'd spiralled so deep into a drug- and whisky-fuelled depression that Siobhan stopped him seeing her for a while. He was so messed up that even that didn't snap him out of it. It was only when, along with Connor, he was charged with murder and spent a few weeks at Walton prison on remand that he finally got his act together. Now he shared custody of his daughter and she was the most important thing in the entire world to him.

'Fuck me, you've got it bad,' Connor chuckled as he came up beside him.

'Knobhead,' Jake replied good-naturedly. 'You sure you're okay to watch her for half an hour?'

'Yeah, but my grandad and Sue are coming. They take Paul to that soft play up the road on a Saturday morning. Isla can go too if she wants.'

'Isn't Paul a bit little for soft play?'

'No, he fucking loves it. Always has a good sleep after too. She can stay here with me and Jazz if she wants, though.'

'Nah, let her go with them. She loves being with Paul,' Jake replied. Isla was in that phase some kids go through where they're obsessed with babies. She adored baby Paul and loved to push his pram and help Jazz dress him.

'Sound. Then I'll have some peace and quiet with the wife,' Connor said with a wicked grin that suggested peace and quiet was the last thing on his mind.

Jake shook his head. 'Fucking animal,' he said with a chuckle.

'Hey. I don't get much kid-free time these days, mate, especially with my dad and your ma gone. I have to take my opportunities where I can.'

'Hmm,' Jake replied, suddenly reminded that he needed a conversation with the two of them.

'You not told her yet?' Connor asked, reading his best mate's mind in the way that he had learned over the years.

'Nope.'

'You want me to tell my dad and then he can tell her? Because if she finds out another way…'

'She won't because only we know, and I'll talk to her later tonight.'

'Well, let me know if you change your mind,' Connor offered as he put an arm around Jake's shoulder.

Chapter Ten

J ake smiled to himself as he sat in his best mate's kitchen and listened to Danny telling Jazz and Connor about the house they'd just viewed. It was a huge five-bed detached with two en-suites, a games room and a gym, and they both loved it. It was a little overpriced in Jake's opinion, but they could certainly afford it, and house prices in the south of Liverpool were constantly rising.

'So, you think you'll put an offer in?' Connor asked.

Danny turned to Jake and smiled. 'Probably, yeah,' he said and Jake nodded his agreement. 'The garden was huge too. We could easily fit a play area for Isla there. She's going to love it.'

'I'll call the estate agents after we've finished our brew. Don't want to look too eager now, do we?' Jake laughed.

'Yes, got to keep the seller on their toes,' Jazz agreed with a smile.

Connor's mobile rang on the table. 'It's my grandad,' he said as he picked it up and held the phone to his ear.

'Everything all right, Grandad?'

Connor's face changed in an instant and Jake's heart started beating faster as he listened to the one-sided conversation. 'Calm down, I can't... Have you looked everywhere? She must be somewhere... Well, why wasn't she...?' Connor's voice got louder and more desperate with each new question he asked Patrick Carter. Everyone in the room stared at him in silent anticipation.

Jake felt a sudden sick feeling in the pit of his stomach. 'What the fuck is going on, Con?' he whispered. Connor turned to him and the look on his face made Jake want to throw up.

'We'll be there in five minutes. Just keep looking for her,' Connor barked and then he ended the call.

'Keep looking for who?' Jake asked but he already knew the answer.

'Isla. They can't find her—'

'What do you mean, they can't fucking find her?' Jake snapped.

'She went off on the play equipment with some of the bigger kids and when Sue went to check on her, she was gone.'

The blood thundered in Jake's ears as he blinked at Connor. This was some kind of mistake. 'She can't just be gone...' he said with a shake of his head. 'She must be there somewhere.'

'She will be, Jake,' Jazz said as she reached across the

table and squeezed his hand in hers. 'Let's get down there and we'll find her.'

Jake nodded and pushed back his chair. Yeah, it was a mistake. Isla was probably playing hide and seek or something. It was a big soft play centre in an old warehouse. Plenty of places for kids to hide. He sucked in a deep breath to try and calm his racing heart.

She's just hiding.

He kept repeating those words over and over to himself like a mantra as he walked out to Connor's car with Danny and Jazz either side of him. Because if he let himself consider an alternative, even for a second, then he might have fallen to the floor and not got back up again.

***

Patrick and Sue were standing outside the soft play centre when Connor's car screeched to a halt outside it ten minutes later. Sue was holding Paul in her arms, but tears were streaming down her cheeks. Patrick looked pale and every day of his sixty-nine years.

Jake jumped out of the car first, with Danny close behind him.

'I'm so sorry, Jake. I only left her for five minutes,' Sue sobbed.

Jake looked past her at the large building, where parents and children were walking around the grounds, some of them calling Isla's name.

'She must be in there,' he said with a frown as he pushed past her.

'She's not, son. We combed through every inch of the place,' Patrick said solemnly just as someone with a Charlie's Play Centre T-shirt came up behind him.

'We've called the police. They're on their way,' she said softly and there was something about the tone of her voice that made the last thread that was holding Jake together snap.

He turned back to Sue and Patrick, his face full of anger and terror, and he did the only thing he knew how to do. He raged. 'How the fuck could you let this happen? You were supposed to be looking after her. You shouldn't have taken your eyes off her for one fucking second!' he shouted, his fists clenched at his sides so he didn't punch Patrick in the face. Sue cried harder as she clung tighter to baby Paul.

'Sir, please…' the employee said, making him turn his attention back to her.

'And what kind of fucking operation do you run here where kids can just walk out…?' he snarled but then the realisation of what else might have happened hit him like someone had taken a baseball bat to his stomach. 'How could you let someone walk in and take her?' he spat the last words out as fast as he could, while he still had the air in his lungs to do it. He felt like his heart was about to give out. Sharp pains seared through his chest and he gasped for breath.

He felt strong hands on his shoulders as Connor and

Danny stood either side of him. 'Breathe, Jake,' Danny said calmly in his ear. 'We'll find her.'

'She's gonna need you at the top of your game, mate,' Connor said quietly in his other ear.

Then Danny's hand was on the back of his neck, steady and calm as he reminded Jake over and over to breathe. He drew in deep breaths, trying to fill his burning lungs with cool air, and as he did, he looked at the anxious and fear-filled faces of the people around him. His daughter was missing. His beautiful little girl was out there somewhere and he had no idea what to do.

Chapter Eleven

D I Kevin Grosvenor swigged the last dregs of his coffee from the cardboard cup and tossed it onto the passenger seat beside him. He hadn't slept a wink since his call from Milo Savage last night and he was running on adrenaline and caffeine. As soon as he'd got to the station that morning, he'd looked up Milo on the PNC. He was a piece of shit. Done a long stretch for a whole bunch of crimes connected to a sex trafficking case and had only been out for a few months. There was no recent intel on him and Kevin had no idea why he needed to get out of the country so quickly, but he would do a little more digging and find out before he handed the man anything that would help him escape. First he needed to know who or what he was escaping from.

Right now, he was on his way to see Nudge Richards and find out how the hell to get his hands on a fake passport. He already had a story to explain his queries. He knew the likes of Nudge would never willingly help the police, but he knew how to apply a little pressure in the right places to secure Nudge's co-operation.

As he was nearing Nudge's scrapyard, a call came through via his Bluetooth. It was from his boss.

'Kev, we've got a kid missing. Possibly a kidnapping. I need you at Charlie's Play Centre on Smithdown retail estate. She was there with her great-grandparents but now hasn't been seen for almost an hour.'

Kevin's heart sank. Those places were usually busting at the seams on a Saturday morning. Who knew how many people had been and gone before the place was locked down.

'The father is there now and the mother is on her way. A squad car is at the scene and Molly is on route. She has all the information that came into the control room.'

'Fuck!' Kevin muttered, both because his trip to see Nudge had been thwarted, but mostly because a kid being kidnapped was awful. Fortunately, it was unusual too. His heart sank. Molly Hadden was his sergeant and she was his best. He was glad she'd be there to deal with this with him, especially as he wasn't exactly on top form.

'Oh, and Kev,' his boss warned. 'I hope you've got your tin hat. This isn't just any kid that's gone missing.'

'Who is she?' Kevin asked with a frown.

'Jake Conlon's daughter.'

'Shit!' Kevin's breakfast threatened to make a sudden reappearance. Given the high profile of her father and her great-grandparents, it was probably a targeted kidnapping.

Which meant that he was going to have to deal with the most ruthless family in the entire city and probably the country while they were dealing with one of their children being taken. It was going to be one long fucking day!

'I know. I want everyone on this, Grosvenor. I need your best team on their A game, because if that lot go on a rampage across my city trying to find this poor kid…' He didn't need to finish his sentence. Kevin was well aware of the possible ramifications.

'I know, Sir.'

'You will report everything to me directly as soon as we have anything at all.'

'Yes, boss.'

'Good. Best of luck,' he said before he ended the call.

Kevin did a U-turn in the middle of Smithdown Road and headed to the retail estate nearby with a heavy heart and the beginnings of a pounding headache.

When Kevin arrived at the soft play centre ten minutes later, his sergeant was waiting outside and there were two squad cars already there. Uniformed officers had cordoned off the area and were walking the grounds, looking for evidence of the missing girl.

He climbed out of his car and walked towards Molly.

'Afternoon, boss,' she said.

'Who's here?' He nodded toward the building behind her.

'Her father, Jake Conlon. The girl's mother, Siobhan Conlon, was at her place of work in Lytham. She's been notified and is on her way.'

'Siobhan Conlon? They're not married still, are they?' Kevin asked with a frown as his eyes swept over the immediate area.

'No, but she never changed her name,' Molly said as she flipped through her notebook.

He noted that there were at least five hundred cars in the car park and surrounding ones. There were two ways in and out of the estate, but they served at least a dozen busy shops and who knew how many cars had been in and out of here in the past few hours. It was unlikely the kidnapper would have travelled on foot if they were taking a child.

'How many more of the family do we have to deal with?' Kevin asked.

'Patrick Carter and his wife, Sue. They were here with Isla when she went missing and they also had their great-grandson, Paul. So his mother, Jasmine Carter, is here...' She stopped talking and Kevin knew why.

'And?'

'Yep. Connor Carter is here too.' She knitted her eyebrows together. 'But from what I've heard so far, they have all been on their best behaviour.'

'Yeah, well, we'll see how long that lasts,' he sighed. Connor Carter was every copper's worst nightmare. Jake Conlon was bad enough, but he was less of a loose cannon than his stepbrother. Connor was reckless and violent, but he was too good at covering his tracks for them to ever get anything on him. Back before his twin had been murdered, it was a well-known fact that the two of them used to travel the length and breadth of the country killing people and disposing of their bodies for the highest bidders. Colloquially known as 'The Cleaners', they had made themselves a fortune by inflicting pain and misery on others. Granted their victims had probably deserved it, but still. Since Paul's murder a few years earlier, Connor had calmed down a little, and now he largely kept his killing and mayhem confined to his own city.

'And one more thing, boss,' she said with a worried look on her face that made him want to turn around, climb into his car and drive back home to bed.

'What?' he asked with a heavy sigh.

'Danny Alexander is here.'

'Fuck!' Kevin ran a hand over his face. He and his team had arrested Danny for murder only a few weeks earlier – a murder he hadn't committed.

'I spoke with him when I got here. Told him we were only doing our jobs and that he needed to put things aside and let us do our jobs now…' she said reassuringly.

'And?'

'He seemed to take it on board. I mean, we all have the same goal, don't we? To find Isla Conlon and get her home safe as soon as possible. He understands that, and while he might hate our guts, I suspect he's going to put his differences to one side, for now at least.'

'Good. Thank you for that,' Kevin said gratefully. Of course there was nothing to worry about. As far as his team and everyone else was aware, they had only been doing their jobs arresting Danny. Nobody else knew that Kevin had always known that he was innocent.

'Has anyone taken statements from the family yet?' he asked as they started to walk up the narrow concrete path leading to the entrance.

'Only from the great-grandparents. No one has spoken to Jake yet. We were waiting for you.'

'How many witnesses do we have?'

Molly sucked the air through her teeth – it was a habit she had when she didn't want to give him bad news.

'Just spit it out, Moll.'

'To be honest, Sir, we don't know.'

'We don't know?'

'We have a list of names of adults who signed in. They have to sign the children in, and give one parent or guardian's details but not all. So if someone came with three kids and three adults, only one adult would have to leave their details. Right now we don't know how many people we potentially need to speak to.'

'What do we know?' he said as he pulled open the glass door and held it for her as she stepped inside. They stopped in the reception area and she flipped over a page of her notebook.

'There are one hundred and eighty-eight customers in here right now. Seventy-six adults and the rest are kids. Twelve members of staff. Isla was last seen by her great-grandparents at approximately ten minutes to twelve. They went to look for her shortly after midday and spent a full fifteen minutes searching the play area before they spoke to staff, who made an announcement. It was another fifteen minutes before they had done a thorough search of the premises and staff decided to call the police.'

'So, we have a potential window of forty-five to fifty minutes when she could have been taken?'

'Yes.'

'How many people left during that time? Can we check the CCTV?'

'There is no CCTV over the door or the whole reception.'

'What? What's the point of having it if you're not going to have it in the right place?'

'No guidelines to say it has to be there, boss. Costs money to have good CCTV in place.'

'But if nothing else, it protects their staff,' he said with a shake of his head.

'This place is renowned for cutting corners. It's staffed by kids fresh out of school, working for minimum wage. Half of it is cash in hand too. You think Charlie gives a crap about their security?'

'Well, he will if Jake Conlon doesn't get his daughter back and he finds out the place has shit security to save a few quid, especially somewhere for kids.'

'Well, let's hope it doesn't come to that, eh?'

'God yes,' he agreed. 'So how do we find out who might have left during this time window?'

'Since the place opened at 9 a.m., one hundred and forty-four adults signed in and three hundred and sixty-kids were paid for. As customers don't have to sign out, we have to assume that any of those people could have been here when Isla went missing.'

Kevin did some quick maths in his head. 'So that's sixty-eight adults we need to find?'

'That we know of, yes.'

'Could be at least double that figure.'

'Yes. But hopefully, by speaking to the parents and guardians who signed in, we can come up with that list pretty quickly.'

Kevin looked inside the huge play centre. 'All those people and nobody saw anyone kidnap an eight-year-old girl?'

'Seems that way,' she replied with a shrug. 'These places are crazy busy though, boss. Especially on a weekend.'

'She must have gone willingly,' Kevin said as he looked at the small electronic gate that prevented people from leaving or entering without a staff member pressing a button to release it. He'd been to plenty of these places with his own kids. They had always seemed perfectly safe, but now he saw how easy it was for people to slip in and out of them unnoticed. 'Which means we're probably looking for a woman?'

'Probably,' Molly agreed. The fact was, a man leaving with a kid who was maybe crying or looking a little lost would just draw more attention. Kids were more likely to trust women. It was what he'd told his own kids. If you're lost and in trouble look for a police officer, a shop worker, or a woman who looks like she could be your nan or your mum.

Kevin nodded to himself as he made mental notes of the gaps he still needed to fill in. 'So, what else do I need to know before I go in there?'

'Call came in just twenty minutes ago. As I said, Isla was with her great-grandparents, Patrick and Sue. She went off to play on the slides. Around twenty minutes later, Gran went to look for her and she wasn't there. They searched the centre and when she couldn't be found they phoned the father and the staff called the police. The father and other family members arrived fifteen minutes ago and nobody has left the building since the call came in to the control room.'

'And we have all of their names?'

'Yes. Even the ones who didn't sign in originally. Uniform are taking their details now.'

Kevin processed the information and developed a checklist in his mind of what needed to be done as a priority. Time was of the essence in these cases. As much as he'd like Molly by his side when he met with the family in a few minutes, she was too valuable an asset to be babysitting him. He would take a constable with him instead.

'Start taking statements from the employees on the desk, but before you do, I want the names of everyone who was here today who is no longer here now. Then I want uniform to work their way through that list. Get me names, addresses. You know the drill, Molly. Let's get this little girl back before teatime, eh?'

'Yes, boss,' she said as they reached a painted wooden door where one of his constables, Caroline Hennessey, was waiting outside. She was new to his team but she was sharp and she was competent. He supposed she was about to really have her mettle tested.

'The family in there?' Kevin asked.

'Yes, Sir.'

'And the centre manager? Where are they at?'

'She's in her office with Mike from uniform, getting the list of names together.'

'And everyone else?'

'In the soft play area, boss. Waiting to be interviewed.'

Kevin nodded. That was a good thing. He'd had visions of Connor and Jake working their way through the room and throttling the life from everyone until they got the information they were looking for.

'Do you have a picture of Isla?'

'Yes, the grandmother sent one that she took of her earlier. So she's even wearing the same outfit.'

'Good. We don't want to keep these people longer than necessary.' He turned back to Molly. 'Get their names. Show them Isla's picture. I want statements from everyone in that room. If they saw anything even slightly suspicious. I want to know who Isla was playing with. Which adults she spoke to. Then let those people go home, but tell them that we may be in touch with further questions. If they're still here they haven't got the girl. We need to focus on the ones that have left. Where are the rest of our team?'

'On their way, boss. Should be here in the next ten minutes.'

'Get them to work as soon as they arrive.'

Molly nodded her understanding. 'And me, boss?' Caroline asked.

'I need someone in there with me.' He nodded to the door. 'You ready to go into the lion's den?'

'Ready when you are,' she said, stepping aside and allowing him to open the door.

Chapter Twelve

J ake looked at the door and waited for someone else to walk through it. Another person to give him some bullshit about how they would find his daughter and he just had to sit here and wait for the police to do their job. How was he supposed to do that? How did a man as powerful as he was just sit around and do nothing while his baby girl was…?

He swallowed the bile in his throat, unable to finish the thought. He saw the weary faces of some of the people as he passed earlier – the other parents who held onto their children for dear life in case some maniac took them away too. They edged away from him, as though it was catching. As if just by being near him they might lose their kids too. Or perhaps they simply knew who he was, and were terrified that he was going to kick the shit out of everyone until someone told him where his daughter was. But the truth was, as much as he felt like doing that, he was shocked into inaction.

He felt like he'd slipped into a coma, his brain synapses no longer firing. Unable to force his brain to think of a better solution, he allowed himself to be told what to do by everyone around him. That copper telling him to sit and wait for her boss. Danny telling him everything was going to be okay and that they would tear the city apart to find Isla. Connor telling him to stay calm until they got some information from the police or anyone else that they could follow up on. He didn't feel calm. He felt angry, terrified and numb at the same time. But he locked the anger and the terror in a tiny little box and kept it closed tight, afraid that if he were to allow himself to feel even a fraction of those emotions, he would drown in them and then he would be no use to anyone.

So, he focused on the numb. Closing his eyes, he was aware of Danny's strong hand on his leg. Jasmine sat beside him, her thigh pressed against his as though she was reminding him she was there for him. Connor was on the phone talking to Luke and organising an operation that would pull every available person from their workforce. He heard Sue crying softly and Patrick comforting her. He didn't even have the energy to ask them why they had been irresponsible enough to allow someone to take his daughter from under their noses. He was sinking into a black hole, his lungs burning with a lack of oxygen, but there wasn't a thing he could do about it.

'Jake!' Danny said and his eyes snapped open. He

looked at the door and recognised the police officer walking through it. It was the inspector who'd had Danny arrested for murder, but even that didn't provoke a reaction in him.

'Mr Conlon,' the DI said as he walked towards him. 'I'm DI Kevin Grosvenor and I'm—'

'I know who you are,' Jake interrupted him.

Grosvenor swallowed hard.

'What are you doing to find Isla?' Danny demanded.

'Everything we can.'

'If you don't have any idea who did this, then give me the names of every person who's been here today and we'll find her our fucking selves,' Connor snarled.

'We have the names of the people who were here today and my team are working to identify anyone who left during the time Isla could have gone missing. I can assure you this is our top priority, but you have to let us do our jobs.'

Connor snorted in derision and Grosvenor sucked in a breath. 'I can't stress enough that you need to let us deal with this investigation, Mr Carter.'

'Yeah, well, maybe I don't give a shit what you think,' Connor snapped as he advanced towards the DI.

Grosvenor squared up to him. 'If any of you do anything to jeopardise this investigation, I will have you arrested and thrown into Walton until this is over. Am I making myself clear?'

'Did you just fucking threaten me?' Connor spat as he edged even closer to DI Grosvenor. Caroline, the constable who was accompanying him, was preparing to force herself between the two men if she had to.

'Connor!' Jake shouted, snapped from his trance. Connor and DI Grosvenor turned and looked at him, giving him their full attention now. 'Sit the fuck down and let him tell us what he knows. We're losing vital time while you two fuck about in a pissing contest.'

'Sorry, mate,' Connor mumbled and then he walked back to the side of the room while DI Grosvenor took a seat.

'The good news is that we have a whole load of witnesses out there, Mr Conlon, and I am confident that at least one of them will have seen or heard something that will tell us where your daughter is.'

'You better be right,' Jake said, glaring at the man in front of him. 'Because you're keeping us locked in here when we should be out there looking for her.'

'You're not being locked in here,' Kevin assured him. 'But we need to make sure we have covered every single angle so that we start off on the best possible footing. So, with that in mind, do you have any idea who might have taken your daughter?'

Jake stared at him. Was he taking the piss? 'If I did, do you think I'd be sitting here waiting for you lot to pull your finger out?'

Kevin took a breath and remained calm. Dealing with hostility was an almost everyday occurrence in his job. 'I know it's difficult, but given who you are—'

'Who I am?' Jake snarled.

Kevin leaned back and rubbed a hand over his jaw. He

was fed up of treading on eggshells. 'I'm going to be honest with you, Jake. Every second counts. We can sit here and pretend that you're the respectable businessman you claim to be, or we can acknowledge that you have probably pissed off more people than the average person, and that the people you deal with aren't particularly moral. Not to mention, you are a very rich man. Now, if there is anyone you can think of whom you may have upset, either recently or even in the distant past, who might want to seek revenge, then it would be helpful if we knew about it.'

Jake swallowed hard. The thought that his little girl was out there in danger somewhere, and that he was the cause of it, was eating him up inside. But his mind was blank. All of his enemies were dead or in prison – except for Milo Savage, but he was after Connor and Jazz. 'No. No one who would do this.'

'Nobody would have known Isla would be here today,' Jazz interrupted, 'if you're thinking this was some kind of premeditated kidnapping. It was a last-minute decision to bring her here, so how would someone have known?'

'Perhaps someone was following you?' Kevin replied.

'Not a chance,' Danny said.

'And what about you, Connor? Your grandparents bring your son here every week, right?'

'Yeah,' he replied, his eyes narrowed in suspicion.

'Is there anyone you can think of? Perhaps they were planning on targeting your son but saw another opportunity when Isla arrived too?'

'No,' Connor snarled.

'Why the fuck would someone take her?' Jake asked, his voice cracking under the pressure.

Nobody answered that particular question, but Kevin turned his attention to the woman sitting beside Patrick Carter. He assumed that it was his wife, Sue. 'Can either of you remember Isla playing with anyone in particular? Mentioning a name? Did you see anyone talking to her?'

Sue opened her mouth to speak but then was overcome by emotion and started to cry again as she shook her head.

'Sue was in the ball pond with Paul. I was sitting having a coffee, can't really get into the play bit with my leg.' He tapped his knee and Kevin nodded. Years earlier, he'd been beaten to a pulp and left for dead. Rumour had been that it was Nathan Conlon who had been responsible but it was never proved and Patrick had never revealed his attacker to the police. 'Isla came over to me and got a drink and then she said she was going to play on the slides. She's too big for the baby part, see. They don't let the big kids in there so she went off to play on her own. She always does that, doesn't she? Plays with the big kids?' He looked to Jazz who nodded her head. 'She's such a confident little thing. She makes friends wherever she goes. She'll play with anyone.'

'But you didn't see her with anyone in particular?'

'No.' Patrick shook his head before he dropped it onto his chest and started to cry.

'And where were you both sitting? Could you see the exit?' Kevin asked.

'No.' He wiped the tears from his face. 'I was by the baby part. You can't see the doors from there.'

'Okay,' Kevin said with a nod. Molly had all the information from the great-grandparents. If Jake and Connor weren't going to divulge anything further, then his time was better spent interviewing the staff and witnesses, and trying to find some CCTV on the estate that would hopefully show at least a part of the play centre's car park.

'Some of my officers will escort you home shortly. I'd like two of them to stay at your house so that they can keep you up to date with all developments, and also in case anyone makes contact with you,' he told Jake.

'Contact?'

'If this was targeted, then whoever took your daughter is likely to be in touch with you.'

'Like a ransom demand or something?' Danny asked.

'Possibly,' Kevin admitted.

'You think someone kidnapped her because of who I am?' Jake asked him and the haunted look in his eyes almost made Kevin want to look away.

'It's a very strong possibility,' he replied before he pushed himself to his feet. 'Caroline here will stay with you. I'll remain in direct contact with her and she'll be able to give you any updates as we receive them.'

'And in the meantime, we just sit and do nothing?' Jake snapped.

'No. You keep thinking of anyone who might have any reason to do something like this, and you allow us to do our jobs.'

'Fucking unbelievable,' Connor muttered under his breath, but Kevin didn't rise to the bait. He didn't have time to massage egos or worry about what might happen if this little girl wasn't found. He had to find Isla Conlon – and fast.

Chapter Thirteen

Siobhan Conlon abandoned her car in front of the entrance to Charlie's Play Centre and started to run inside.

'Miss,' a uniformed police officer said as he stepped out in front of her.

'My daughter is missing,' she shouted at him, unable to believe the words even as they came out of her mouth.

'Let her through,' a woman said. Siobhan assumed she was a police officer, although she was dressed in everyday clothes. Taking Siobhan by the arm, the woman escorted her inside.

'Where is my daughter?' Siobhan demanded, her voice cracking with the effort of trying to keep her emotions in check. 'Where is Isla?'

'We're doing everything we can to find her as soon as possible, Ms Conlon.'

'But who? How?' Siobhan wailed as the reality of the

situation slowly started to sink in. On the drive back from Lytham she had broken every speed limit possible and gone through at least two red lights, but the whole time she'd convinced herself that what Jake had told her wasn't really possible. Somehow he was mistaken. It was another child. She had convinced herself that she'd get here and Isla would come running into her arms laughing about what a funny joke she'd played. But now, seeing the police cars and the uniforms and the looks on their faces – that was the worst of it. The way they were all looking at her.

'Your ex-husband and some of his family are here, Ms Conlon,' the woman said softly as she guided her into a small room.

The first person Siobhan saw was Jake. He was sitting with his head in his hands, his shoulders slumped in defeat. Like he was broken. Why wasn't he tearing the city apart already to find their daughter? Why didn't he have his own personal army out there searching for their little girl? Instead, he was just sitting there. Doing nothing.

But then he looked up at the sound of her coming into the room and when she saw his face, her heart broke in two. He couldn't do any of those things right now, because he was broken – just like she was.

'Jake,' she cried as she took a step towards him. He stood up and wrapped his arms around her and she sagged against his chest and sobbed. There was no one else in this room, in this world, who knew what they were going through. No one else could even come close to comprehending the sheer paralysing terror that had an icy grip on her heart, except this man right here.

———

Jazz caught Danny's eye and indicated the doorway, where Connor was already standing. Siobhan and Jake were busy talking to the police. It was the perfect time to come up with a plan of action of their own. Jake, understandably, seemed to have been rendered useless with the shock and worry of his daughter being missing, which was why it was up to her and the rest of the family to do what needed to be done.

Danny glanced at Jake, checking he wasn't needed, before standing and following Jazz and Connor out of the small room, which had now become overcrowded and stuffy. Jazz noted the police officers eyeing them warily as they passed, making their way outside to find a private space to talk.

'Is there something I can help you with?' an officer in uniform said as they stepped into the car park.

'No, thanks. Just getting some air,' Jazz replied coolly.

The officer stepped aside and allowed them to pass while still keeping a watchful eye on the three of them as they made their way to Connor's car and stood beside it.

'We need to start looking for Isla. Now,' Jazz said.

'Yeah,' Danny agreed as he glanced back at the police officers swarming the scene. 'That lot are fucking useless, let's face it.'

'Do either of you have any idea who might have taken her?' she asked the two men.

Both shook their heads. 'No one who would do this. I mean, we're still looking for Milo, but…' Connor scrubbed a hand over his jaw.

'I don't see why he would take Isla,' Danny added. 'It's you two he's got a beef with. Not Jake.'

'I know,' Jazz said, her eyebrows knitted as she racked her brain to think of any other potential enemies. She couldn't, though – at least none that would go as far as to kidnap a child. Then a horrible thought occurred to her, one that made her blood turn to ice in her veins. 'Your grandad and Sue have been bringing Paul here every Saturday for the past two months,' she said to her husband.

'Yeah?'

'What if Isla was never the target? Nobody knew that she would be there today. If this is about revenge and who we are, then it must have been planned. What if they really intended to take Paul, but they saw Isla instead and figured she was an easier target?' Even as she said the words, Jazz felt like a knife had been plunged into her chest. The thought of anything happening to her child was the worst possible thing she could ever imagine.

'So maybe it *was* something to do with Milo then?' Connor snarled, his handsome features distorted in a scowl and his fists balled by his side.

Danny sucked in a breath. 'It would be the perfect way to hurt you both. And we already know there's no lines he wouldn't cross.'

Connor's jaw clenched and a vein bulged in his temple. Jazz could feel the anger in him like the heat from an open fire. But his anger was good. It would fuel his efforts to find Milo, and hopefully Isla, as fast as possible. Jazz could barely imagine the fear and worry that Jake and Siobhan were experiencing right now. They all had to pull together to fix this and bring her niece home.

'We don't tell the bizzies anything about this,' Connor hissed.

'Agreed,' Jazz said.

'How the fuck do we get out of here without them getting on to what we're doing, though?' Danny asked. 'You know they're all watching us, right? Waiting for one of us to make a move.'

'You and Connor stay here for now. Play the comforting partner and uncle. They should let us go home soon and as soon as they do, you two do what you need to do to find Milo. In the meantime, we'll tell Luke and John our concerns but we have them focus on the people who were here this morning. We can't know for sure it was him, and if it was, then he wouldn't have been stupid enough to come here himself. He must have had an accomplice.'

Danny nodded his agreement. 'I'll call Luke now,' he said, taking his mobile from his coat pocket and dialling his best mate's number. He stepped away, leaving Jazz and Connor alone for a few moments.

'If it is him and he really was after Paul, I don't want us going back to the house,' Connor said.

'We could use your dad and Grace's place as a base for

now. It's bigger and they'll be on their way back as soon as they find out what's happened.'

'Hmm.' Connor nodded his agreement but his mind was clearly elsewhere.

'We'll find him,' Jazz said, placing a reassuring hand on his forearm. 'And Isla too.'

'If he hurts her, Jazz...' He shook his head.

'I know,' she whispered. She felt the guilt too. That her niece might have been kidnapped because of her made her feel like she couldn't breathe. But there was also the guilt of the relief she felt that it wasn't her own child who'd been taken. She knew Connor would be feeling exactly the same.

'Luke is going to fill John in and they're going to start making some enquiries about this place and who was here this morning. We can bring in every person we have if we need to,' Danny said as he walked back to where they were standing.

Jazz nodded. 'You think we should keep our suspicions about Milo to ourselves for now?'

'Why?' Danny asked with a frown.

'You saw Jake in there, Danny. He's broken.'

'Fucking understandable when you consider some sick fucker has probably kidnapped his daughter, Jazz,' he snapped at her.

She sensed the increasing tension in Connor as he stood beside her. Emotions were running high. Ordinarily Danny would never speak to her like that, and Connor certainly wouldn't allow it, but these weren't ordinary circumstances.

Taking hold of his hand, she squeezed gently, silently letting him know that she had everything in control.

'I know, Danny,' she said softly. 'I know I'd be the same if it was Paul who'd been taken. All I'm trying to say is that maybe we don't burden him with the worry of Milo having taken Isla if we can help it. I mean, maybe she did wander off on her own? Maybe there's another explanation that is not as terrifying as the one where she was taken by *him*.' She spat the last word. Milo Savage was certainly living up to his name. She could hardly believe she had once cared for him even the tiniest fraction. The fact that she had allowed him to touch her made her want to scrub her skin with bleach.

Danny glared at her and Connor. 'I'm not lying to his face. I don't care how guilty you two might feel,' he snapped, revealing a level of insight that people often underestimated in him. 'I won't bring it up but if he asks me I'm gonna tell him the truth.'

'Okay. I suppose that's fair enough.' She glanced at her husband, who still looked like he wanted to punch Danny in the face, but she needed the two of them to work together more than ever on this. She squeezed Connor's hand again. 'Jake and Isla need both of you more than ever right now,' she reminded them.

'I know. As soon as we can get out of here, me and Connor will find her.'

'Yeah,' Connor agreed and just like that, they were all on the same page again.

Chapter Fourteen

Grace Carter tilted her face toward the sun and smiled as she lay on the soft padded sun lounger. She and Michael and their two youngest children had been in Spain for two months now. It had been difficult at first to take that step back and allow their oldest sons to take control of their empire back in Liverpool. When they'd first arrived here, Michael had made her promise to limit herself to one phone call home per day. It had been tough not to constantly call and check how they were doing, especially as she knew both Jake and Connor would be too proud to ask for help even if they needed it, but Michael reminded her how far their sons had come in the past few years. Whilst they both still had a reckless and ruthless streak, they had matured into good businessmen too. They had young families of their own to take care of, and she consoled herself with the fact that they would do all they could to keep themselves and her grandchildren safe. Not to mention her daughter-in-law, Jazz, was also running things now. Grace was sure Jazz would never let anything get too out of hand before she let her know there was something going on.

So now Grace was finally able to switch off a little and relax. She and Michael were overseeing the construction and opening of a new seafront restaurant, but it didn't require a lot of oversight and they got plenty of time for themselves and to spend with their youngest two children, Belle and Oscar. Even though she still kept busy, this life felt very close to the retirement that she and Michael had spoken of.

Speaking of her handsome husband, she pulled her sunglasses down the bridge of her nose as the sound of water caught her attention. She watched as he climbed out of their pool and made his way toward her. His swim shorts clung to his muscular thighs and water dripped off his tanned, toned muscles. Her stomach fluttered at the sight of him. Even after all these years she still couldn't get enough of him. To the outside world he might be one of the most dangerous and terrifying men they had ever met, but to her he was the most supportive and loving man she had ever known. He was the kind of husband she had once only dreamed about having. He made her and their children his number-one priority every single second of every single day, and that made him the sexiest man alive in her eyes.

As he reached her, he brushed his wet hair back from his face before flicking water at her. The cold droplets landed on her hot skin.

'Michael,' she squealed as he came closer until he was

crawling over her and soaking her with pool water. 'You're getting me soaking wet.'

'That's kind of the idea,' he said with a wicked grin as he nudged her knees apart and lay between her thighs before kissing her softly.

'I was just about to read my book.'

'I can think of far more interesting things to do than read while we have the place to ourselves,' he chuckled darkly as one hand coasted down her body making goosebumps prickle along her forearms.

'You need to get yourself some new hobbies, because that is all you ever think about,' she said with feigned indignation, but she couldn't help smiling as her insides contracted in anticipation.

'What is the point of wearing this tiny little bikini if not to drive your husband completely crazy?' he growled as he tugged at the tie on the bottoms. It came undone easily in his hand.

'I wanted to work on my tan,' she giggled as she squirmed beneath him while he tugged on the tie at the other side.

Grace bit her lip as she watched the confusion flicker over his face. He looked down at his hands. 'What fucking devious trickery is this?' he growled as her bikini bottoms remained firmly in place.

'The ties are just for show,' she laughed.

'What the fuck?' He shook his head in exasperation and she laughed harder. 'I'll just take them off you the old-fashioned way then.' He arched an eyebrow at her as he pushed himself up onto his knees.

'Michael!' She pulled him back down until he was lying on her again. 'We can't here. Someone might come back.'

Michael's brother, Sean, along with his wife, Sophia, were visiting. They were involved with the restaurant too, and they had taken Belle and Oscar out to the local horse-riding centre for the morning.

He frowned at her. 'You do remember our children? The two loudest individuals on the entire planet?'

'They are not,' she said as she swatted him on the chest.

'We'll hear them all if they come home. Trust me. Have I ever led you astray?'

'Yes. Many, many times,' she laughed as he brushed her hair back from her face.

'Stop talking, Mrs Carter,' he growled before he sealed his lips over hers and kissed her deeply. He rocked his hips against hers until she could feel his hardness against her groin and all of her excuses suddenly became less important as she wrapped her arms around his neck.

The sound of *Z Cars* started playing loudly in their ears and Grace glanced sideways at her phone on the small table beside her. She had a different ringtone for each of the people important to her, and that one signalled Jake was calling. It wasn't entirely unusual for him to call her during the day, but it was ordinarily her who called him. It made the hairs on the back of her neck stand on end – or perhaps that was Michael's wandering hands?

'Leave it. He'll call back later,' he mumbled as he started to trail soft kisses over her jaw and down to her throat.

'Okay,' she whispered as she ran her hands through his thick dark hair. A few seconds later the tune stopped and Grace relaxed in her husband's arms. She hated ignoring her son's calls, but she'd ring him back soon. Besides, if it was important he'd call straight back.

When the sound of *Z Cars* filled the air again Michael stopped kissing her and looked at the phone with concern in his eyes. Grace's pulse raced as she reached for her phone and pressed it to her ear.

Michael pushed himself up and stared at her as she answered.

'Jake? Is everything okay?'

'Mum!' The terror and panic in his voice was so apparent that Grace felt her heart stop beating in her chest. 'Mum!' he said again, almost crying out the word.

'What is it, son?' she asked, willing him to tell her so she could stop imagining the worst. Michael squeezed her free hand tightly in his and she was grateful for his calm and reassuring presence.

Jake's words didn't stop her imagining the worst – because they were more terrifying than any others he could have spoken. 'Someone has taken Isla.'

Grace hurried around the villa throwing random things into bags but she had no idea what she had or hadn't packed.

Jake hadn't been able to give her much information. He'd been far too distraught to even speak but then Danny had taken the phone and given her a summary of the information they had. It had now been two hours since Isla had disappeared.

Given who Jake was, the police weren't ruling out a targeted kidnapping, but as yet there had been no contact from any kidnappers and no ransom demand. All she could think of was the fact that some psychopath had her beautiful, sweet, innocent granddaughter. Oh, God. Poor Isla. What would be going through her little head? She'd be terrified. Crying for her mum and dad. Grace blinked away the tears. She could hardly breathe thinking about what her granddaughter might be going through – and what if they were hurting her? What if…?

Her knees buckled under her and she felt herself falling to the floor before she was caught by two strong arms wrapping around her waist.

'We'll get her back, Grace. I promise,' Michael soothed in her ear as he pressed her tight to his chest.

Grace sagged against her husband, tears running down her cheeks as she battled with the emotions running through her head. Michael held onto her. He wasn't used to seeing his strong, capable wife like this. She was usually the one holding everybody else together. But he knew Jake's phone call had rocked her to her very core. Her biggest fear in life was anything happening to their children or grandchildren. It was his too, but he had to hold it together for her right now. It was one of the reasons they worked so well together as a couple – when one of them crumpled, the other held them up.

'What if we don't?' she whispered, her voice trembling as she spoke.

He cupped her chin in his hand, tilting her face until she was looking into his eyes. 'Hey! Have I ever let you down?'

'No.' She shook her head gently.

'And I never will. Okay? Our flight is leaving in three hours. Sean is on his way back with the kids. In less than eight hours we'll all be back in Liverpool and we will find Isla. I promise you.'

She nodded as she swallowed hard and he wiped the tears from her cheeks with the pads of his thumbs. He needed her to be strong. As much as he loved looking after her, he needed his warrior wife back. As powerful as he and his brother were, and their father before them, they had nothing on this woman. Grace Carter was the one person who could fix this and they needed her to be at the top of her game.

He narrowed his eyes at her. 'I can't do this without you, Grace.'

She sucked in a deep breath as she looked into his eyes, her back straightening slightly. He hated that he couldn't let her feel what she needed to, but it wouldn't do any of them any good. 'I know,' she said with a sniff and then she looked around the room. 'Where are Sean and Sophia with the kids? They should be back by now.'

'They're five minutes away.'

'I can't find our passports.' She looked over his shoulder at the things strewn across the room.

'They're in the safe. I'll get them.'

'I need to pack. We need…' She trailed off.

'We have everything we need at home, Grace.'

She nodded again. 'Okay.'

'You want to call Jake again?'

'No.' She shook her head. 'He'll call if he has any news. I'll just be distracting him. You think I should call Siobhan though?'

Michael narrowed his eyes at her. Michael wasn't Siobhan's biggest fan. She'd had a one-night stand with his son, Connor, shortly before she got pregnant with Isla and it had caused an almighty rift in their family. He couldn't stay pissed off with his son about it for ever, so he chose to blame Siobhan instead. But right now he could think of nothing but how much pain the woman must be in.

'I don't think that's a good idea. Wait until we're home and you can speak to her face to face, okay?'

'Yes. Of course. You're right,' she admitted with a sigh. 'If it was to do with us though, and who we are, why hasn't anyone been in touch yet, Michael? Why haven't they asked for anything? Money or whatever the hell is it they want?'

'I don't know, love,' he replied with a shake of his head.

Grace swallowed the bile that rushed from her stomach and burned the back of her throat. She suspected that she knew the answer and it terrified her. It was because whoever had taken her granddaughter didn't want money or anything else. They simply wanted Isla.

That thought seemed to snap her from her panic-induced haze. Michael was right. They all needed her more than ever right now. This wasn't the time for falling apart. It was the time for doing what she did best.

'I need to call Leigh,' Grace said as she stepped back from Michael. While she waited for the kids to get back so they could all travel to the airport, she needed to do something useful to keep her occupied.

Michael handed her her mobile phone from the table beside them.

Chapter Fifteen

D I Leigh Moss was briefing her team on their latest case when she saw the familiar name flashing on her mobile phone on the table in front of her. She had been expecting this ever since she'd received the news that Isla Conlon was missing. The whole station was abuzz with it. It wasn't every day the daughter of Merseyside's most notorious gangster was kidnapped. And whilst her colleagues might prefer to assist Lucifer himself rather than Jake Conlon and the rest of the Carter family, there was no such prejudice when a child was involved.

The Major Incident Team were handling the case. Leigh had wondered how that would work given that DI Grosvenor had been the one who had led the investigation into Glenda Alexander's murder a few weeks earlier, and wrongfully charged Danny. But she supposed that, given the gravity of the whole situation, both parties could put aside their differences and work together.

'Mark, can you take over? I need to take this,' she asked her sergeant.

'Of course, Ma'am,' he replied, taking her place and continuing with the brief, allowing Leigh to slip out of the room.

'Hi, Grace,' Leigh said as she answered the call. They hadn't parted on the best of terms the last time they spoke. In fact, Grace had called her a bitch and thrown her out of her house, but Leigh wasn't hard-hearted enough to hold that against the woman right now.

'Hi, Leigh.' The crack in her voice was audible and she took a deep breath before she continued talking. 'Do you know anything yet?'

That was it. No pleasantries. No words of apology or small talk. But that was their relationship. Leigh gave a wry smile as she realised that no matter what they went through in life, the two of them would always be there for each other when they really needed it, and as illogical as it seemed, she found a strange sense of comfort in that.

'Not yet, Grace. Our MIT are dealing with the case, and they are the best at what they do,' she assured her, because despite Kevin Grosvenor's fuck-up regarding Glenda's murder, he and his team were professional and experienced. And when a child was missing, it pulled at something in everyone. It made everyone go over and above – no matter who the child's father was. 'But if I hear anything helpful at all, I will let you know.'

'Thanks,' Grace said with a soft sigh.

'In this case, though, the police are working with your family, remember? They will give you all of the information you need. They won't hold anything back. You all have the same goal here.'

'Hmm. I guess I never experienced that before.'

'We'll get her back,' Leigh assured her.

'From what Danny told me, they suspect some kind of ransom might be asked for?'

'Well, given Jake's—' Leigh paused, unsure of the correct word for the situation, '—reputation,' she finally settled on, 'that's understandable. That would be my first line of inquiry.'

'But there's been no contact yet. Wouldn't they have made contact by now?'

'It depends. But these kinds of cases aren't my speciality, Grace. DI Grosvenor and his team will be alert to anything like that coming in.'

'Hmm,' Grace mumbled absent-mindedly.

'I assume you're coming back to Liverpool?'

'Yes. Our flight leaves in a few hours.'

'Well, I guess I'll see you when you get back,' Leigh said.

'Yes. Thank you, Leigh.'

'Bye, Grace.'

Leigh placed her phone in her pocket and headed back into the briefing room. She allowed Sergeant Whitney to carry on with the presentation while her mind wandered. Who the hell would want to kidnap Isla Conlon? And was it a targeted attack, or simply an opportunist one? Was the perpetrator looking for any child, or were they specifically wanting Isla? It would be a hell of a coincidence if it was the former, and Leigh didn't believe in coincidences.

Chapter Sixteen

D anny wrapped his arms around Jake's neck and
hugged him tightly. He wished he could shoulder
some of the pain for him. He was sick with worry about Isla
and terrified of what might happen if they didn't get her
back, but he realised it all paled into insignificance in
comparison to what Jake and Siobhan must be feeling. 'I'll
see you at your mum's in a few hours. Call me if you need
me, though, and I'll be right there, okay?'

'Yeah,' Jake mumbled as he clung to him. There was a
part of Danny that wanted to stay and comfort the man he
loved more than anyone else in the world, but he couldn't
sit around feeling helpless and hopeless. He could hardly
bear to look at poor Siobhan, who looked like she was about
to crumple at any second. She hovered behind Jake, waiting
for him to walk to the car with her. She had been clinging to
him from the moment she arrived and Danny understood
why. Her ex-husband was the closest thing to her daughter

she had right now. He'd been told that she'd never been that close to her own parents, who'd emigrated to Australia about a year earlier, leaving her with no other family to rely on but Jake. But still, it hurt him a little to see them together and feel like he was the outsider. Besides all of that, if he sat still for too long and thought about what might be happening to the little girl he'd come to love so much, he might just crumple himself.

'Come on, Dan,' Connor said in his ear as he placed his large hand on the top of Jake's head – letting him know that he was there for him too. But Connor was like Danny – he couldn't wait around for something to happen and especially not now that he suspected Milo might be the man responsible. Besides, Connor Carter trusted the police less than anyone else Danny knew. He had no confidence at all that they would find Isla and bring her home.

'I'll ring you as soon as we find out anything,' Danny said as he pulled back from Jake.

'Find her, Dan,' Jake said, his eyes brimming with tears as he pleaded with him.

'I will,' Danny promised. 'I will.'

Danny climbed into the passenger seat of Connor's car, looking back at the sea of faces as they pulled out of the car park.

'Anyone following us?' Connor asked.

'Not yet, mate. Think they're all too preoccupied with other stuff.'

'Useless pricks,' Connor snarled.

'Yeah,' Danny agreed. He'd never been the biggest fan of Merseyside Police, but ever since they'd had him thrown into Walton prison for his own mother's murder, his opinion of them had only got lower. 'You got any ideas where to start then?' he asked, hoping that Connor knew where they were going, because so far all leads to the elusive Milo Savage had been dead ends.

'Gonna revisit some people we already spoke to,' he snapped and Danny's heart sank. Connor and Jake were incredibly skilled in getting information from people even if they were determined not to give it. He doubted the two of them had missed something in the people they'd already interrogated. 'And I'm waiting on a call from Jerrod King too,' Connor added with a knowing grin.

That certainly got Danny's attention. Jerrod and his brother Devlin had murdered Danny's mum and Jerrod was on remand in HMP Liverpool for the crime. Jazz had shot Devlin and Danny and Luke had disposed of his body somewhere they were sure it would never be found. But both of the King brothers had been working for Milo Savage. Up until now, any efforts to speak to Jerrod had been thwarted by the fact that he was in the segregation unit for his own protection – not only had he crossed the biggest firm in Merseyside, but he'd also raped an old woman. He had a pretty big target on his back. And whilst

Jake and Connor had pull in the prison, they couldn't get a prisoner out of seg – at least not until now.

'How did you swing that?' Danny asked him.

'Pulled in every fucking favour that we have, lad,' he said with a sigh. 'But we should get to speak to him soon.'

'And what about his crew of feral gobshites? You think any of them knew anything about Milo?'

'Couldn't hurt to ask. If we can find any of them, that is. They seem to have disbanded now their leaders have disappeared.'

'I reckon if we go asking round that estate we'll find a few of them though,' Danny suggested. 'Shall we head there first?'

'Sounds like a plan,' Connor agreed, turning onto Smithdown Road and heading towards the north of the city.

Danny winced as Connor plunged the screwdriver into the lad's ear. That had to hurt like a motherfucker. Lincoln Halley, one of the former chief henchmen of the King brothers, howled in pain as the blood trickled down his face. Connor Carter was skilled at causing pain and not even flinching while he did it.

They had found Lincoln selling weed out of an old Ford Fiesta on the Bridewell estate where he and his former bosses once used to rule with fear and intimidation. It was quite a comedown for him. Connor had dragged him out of the car and now had him pressed against the side of it, and not one person around there batted an eyelid when they passed and saw the scene unfolding before them. The Bridewell Blades crew were hated – every last one of them. They had caused nothing but misery for the residents for the past two years and Danny was sure that everyone, apart from the crew themselves, was glad their reign was well and truly over.

'I don't fucking believe you, Lincoln. You're telling me you never once met this prick?'

Lincoln tried to press his hand to his ear to stop the bleeding and suppress the pain, but Connor wouldn't allow him. Instead he pressed his own thumb into Lincoln's already wounded ear and the lad made a noise the like of which Danny had never heard before.

'Argh!' he screamed, about ready to pass out, but for the fact that Connor kept applying pressure and causing enough pain to keep him conscious. 'I didn't. I swear.'

'What do you think?' Connor turned and looked at him.

'I don't think he has the balls to take that kind of pain if he's lying, mate,' Danny replied with a shrug. Now that Devlin and Jerrod were out of the picture, their former crew had revealed themselves to be nothing but cowards and bullies. They had no loyalty to their one-time leaders, and he suspected that they had even less to Milo Savage, who was proving himself to be one of the most slippery cunts Danny had ever had the displeasure of dealing with.

'Huh.' Connor grunted his agreement, pushing Lincoln to the floor and allowing the lad to hold onto his wounded ear. He gave Lincoln a final kick in the shins for his trouble before walking back to Danny, who was leaning against Connor's silver Mercedes.

'So where now?' Danny asked.

Connor ran a hand through his thick dark hair. 'Fuck knows, Dan. Short of torturing every single person who has ever spoken to Savage, I'm fucking stuck, mate. And we don't exactly have time for that. I mean, what if it's not even anything to do with him?'

Danny nodded in agreement. They needed more information on who'd been at that soft play centre when Isla was taken – and they needed it now.

'I'll call Luke and see if they're having any luck,' he suggested.

'Yeah,' said Connor as they both climbed into the car.

Before Danny could call Luke, Connor's phone began to ring. He started the engine and the call connected to the Bluetooth in his car so that Danny could hear it too.

'Mr Carter, I have someone here you'd like to have a word with.' A thick Scottish accent came through the speakers.

'About fucking time, Mick,' Connor muttered under his breath.

'Speak to him, dickhead,' Mick snapped and a few seconds later, the incredibly annoying voice of Jerrod King filled the car instead.

'What do you want?' he drawled.

'Do you have any idea where Milo Savage is?' Connor asked.

'Like I'd tell you if I did,' he snorted.

'Mick?' Connor said and the sound of Jerrod yelping in pain filled the car.

'Do you?' Connor asked again.

'No. Do you know where my brother is?' Jerrod whined.

'Do you have any addresses for him? Any places he stayed? People he stayed with?'

'What? I wasn't his fucking secretary.' Jerrod laughed at his own joke.

'For fuck's sake, Mick,' Connor snarled.

Sounds of scuffling and grunting could be heard, followed by Mick's snarling. 'If you don't speak to Mr Carter with the respect that he deserves, you'll be eating through a straw for the next five years, you little shit. Now tell him what he wants to know.'

'I didn't know anything like that. He only ever met us in Liverpool,' Jerrod finally admitted, his tone still dripping with contempt.

'If I find out you're lying to me, you little prick, you won't make it to your trial. Segregation or not. You understand me?'

'I don't fucking know nothing,' Jerrod insisted.

'Sorry, Mr Carter, I got to get this little fucker back to his cell.'

'Yeah. Thanks, Mick,' Connor said before ending the call.

'I'll call Luke. See if he has anything we can follow up on. I can't face going back to the house with nothing,' Danny suggested.

Connor sighed deeply. 'I know, mate. We own this fucking city, so let's start reminding people of that, eh?'

Chapter Seventeen

Kevin Grosvenor wiped the bead of sweat from his brow as he walked out of the incident room. Their search for CCTV hadn't yielded much result yet, given how many people used that retail park on a busy Saturday morning. He had no idea how, in such a technological age, they were unable to get some footage of the play centre's entrance. He wondered if the kidnapper was aware of that fact. Did he or she know that there were no working cameras? Could it possibly be an inside job?

His personal phone rang in his pocket, snapping him from his thoughts. He took it out, expecting it to be his wife and to have to tell her he wouldn't be home for dinner, but his heart sank when he saw the unknown number. He contemplated not answering it, but he knew it would only continue to ring.

Pressing the button to take the call, he held the phone to his ear.

'Have you got me what I need yet?' Milo Savage barked into his ear.

Kevin's already high blood pressure almost shot through the roof. He would have thought someone in such desperate need of a favour from him would show a little more respect. But he didn't have it in him to get into that right now. He walked into his office and closed the door.

'Not yet. It's going to take a little longer than expected.'

'You useless fucking—' Milo started to rant down the phone, but Kevin cut him off before he could really begin.

'Look, you demanding piece of shit,' he hissed. 'You are not the only problem I have right now.'

'I'm your most dangerous one though,' Milo snarled.

'I wouldn't count on it,' Kevin snorted.

'Just get me what I need and I'll be out of your hair.'

'I wish it was that easy,' Kevin replied with a sigh. 'I will sort it. Just give me a few more days. I just got landed with a massive case and it is going to take every second of my time, but as soon as I get a chance, I'll get you what you need.'

'What case? You have cases all the fucking time, why is this different?' Milo demanded.

'Because it is quite possibly going to get me killed if I don't handle it right,' he snapped. 'Just give me a few more days. Okay?' He ended the call without waiting for Milo to answer. Leaning back in his chair, he took a deep breath and looked out of his office window and across the city. *Where are you, Isla Conlon?*

Chapter Eighteen

His hands curled into fists, Milo Savage punched the door as the anger and frustration surged through his veins like it was his lifeblood. The cheap timber crunched under his hand and he left a hole in the wood so big that he could see right through to the kitchen.

'Fucking cunt,' he snarled as he pulled his hand back, barely even registering the splinters of wood or his bleeding knuckles. He held onto his phone in his other hand. It felt like it was his only lifeline these days. He hated being holed up in this flat, but the reality of his situation was not lost on him. He had no friends left. They were all dead, in jail, or they'd disowned him as soon as he wasn't any use to them anymore – just like that bitch Jasmine had. As time ticked on, he was starting to realise that she was just as bad as the rest of them. She had played him for a fool.

He needed to leave the country. He had eighty grand in

an offshore account. It was enough for him to start over –
somewhere hot and sunny, where nobody knew his name.

He'd consider the risk of using his own passport if he
had one, but his had run out while he was in prison. And
while there were no warrants out for his arrest, he was on
licence, and given the offences he'd been arrested for, he
couldn't be sure he wouldn't flag up on some system if he
did try and leave while using his own name. Still, he was
getting so desperate, he'd be prepared to give it a try. He
was phoning his probation officer every few days, feeding
her some bullshit story about having the flu that bought
him a couple of weeks with no face-to-face appointment,
but soon she would want to see him. He couldn't risk
showing up at the probation office. He'd be a sitting duck if
he did. That prick Connor Carter would no doubt have
some of his goons on the lookout, waiting to pounce.

He scrolled through the few contacts in his phone and
dialled the number of the only other friend he had –
considering himself pathetic that this was the case even as
he did it.

'What is it now?' Barrow asked with a sigh as he
answered the call.

'That prick Grosvenor still hasn't sorted me out,' he
snapped. 'You know anyone else who can help me? Because
he seems a bit tied up with other shit.'

'Oh? What other shit?'

'Said he's working on some big case.'

He heard Barrow laughing softly and frowned. *Devious
fucker!*

'Did he say what kind of case?'

'No. Only that it could get him killed if he didn't handle it right,' Milo snapped. 'Can you help me out or not?'

'I am helping you, Milo,' Barrow replied and Milo could almost see the smug grin on his face. He thought he was so fucking clever.

'What the fuck are you on about?'

'Let's just say, I'm dealing with your problem. You might not even need to leave the country if Grosvenor does his job properly.'

Milo snorted a laugh. 'I won't hold my breath then.'

'He might come across as a bit obtuse, but he's a good DI,' Barrow assured him.

'I don't really give a fuck. I want out of this shit-hole country. I need a fucking passport.'

'Then wait for Kevin to get you one. He'll come through. Just sit tight.'

'Easy for you to say.'

The line went dead and Milo scowled at the phone in his hand. He had no idea what the hell Barrow had pulled now, but if Grosvenor didn't come up with the goods soon, he'd have to start tightening the screws.

Chapter Nineteen

J azz handed her son to his great-grandfather Pat to take him for his bath.

'Be good for Grandpa,' she whispered, giving her son a soft kiss on his head. Her heart felt like it was being constricted in a vice as she looked at his beautiful smiling face. If anything ever happened to him...

'Thanks, love,' Pat said, the words catching in his throat, and when Jazz looked up at him, his eyes were brimming with tears. She couldn't even imagine the guilt he and Sue were feeling. They had hardly spoken to Jake and Siobhan since they'd all got back to Grace and Michael's house a few hours earlier. She suspected they didn't know what to say to make the situation any better. There were no words, after all. The only thing they could do to make everything right again was get Isla back, and she knew that Connor, Danny, Luke, John and at least two dozen of their best employees were out there trying their best to make that happen. Pat seemed thankful for being given something to do, and Jazz was happy to be able to focus on her efforts at co-ordinating the search as best she could while keeping an eye on Jake and Siobhan.

Jazz watched Pat talking to her son as he carried him up the stairs, then she turned and headed back to the kitchen to see Jake and Siobhan sitting at the island where she'd left them ten minutes before. Jake held onto Siobhan's hand and the two of them sat staring into space.

'Any news yet?' Jazz asked one of the two uniformed police officers who had accompanied them home and who DI Grosvenor had insisted stay at the house.

'No,' she replied with a solemn shake of her head. 'You?'

Jazz shook her head too before walking over to the distraught parents.

'Where's Danny?' Jake asked when he saw Jazz.

'He's out looking for Isla with Connor. He'll be back soon,' she reassured him.

'I should get out there and look for her too,' he said, pushing his stool back and standing up.

'It would be best if you stayed here,' the police officer said softly. 'In case anyone tries to contact you, or Isla comes home?'

'This isn't her home,' Siobhan said, blinking in confusion as she stared at the woman who had just spoken.

'We have two of our men waiting at your house too, Siobhan,' Jazz said as she placed a reassuring hand on Siobhan's shoulder. 'If she goes home then we'll know about it straightaway, okay?'

'I can't just sit here though,' Jake said, running a hand through his hair. 'It's driving me fucking mad not being able to do anything.'

'Jake!' Siobhan sobbed, reaching for him as soon as he strayed from her.

'Siobhan needs you right now. I promise you Connor and Danny are doing everything they can,' Jazz said pointedly, but everyone in the room knew what that meant. The police had asked questions about where Connor and Danny went when they left the soft play centre, but they had every right to go looking for Isla, and even if the police suspected they were going about it with their usual disregard for the law, there wasn't much they could do about it unless they caught them in the act. DI Grosvenor had warned them all not to do anything to jeopardise the investigation and they had all sworn that they wouldn't. The thing was, his idea of them jeopardising the investigation was their way of getting things done.

'What the fuck are you lot even doing to find her?' Jake barked at the two uniformed officers as he sat down again.

'Finding your daughter is our top priority right now, Mr Conlon,' the officer replied.

Jake snorted in derision as he took hold of Siobhan's hand again and the two of them went back to sitting quietly together, each of them lost in their own private hell.

Jazz checked her mobile phone for what felt like the hundredth time that hour. There was still no update. She had spoken to Connor two hours ago and he had told her that he and Danny were focusing on finding Milo and had a few leads to chase up, but she hadn't heard from him since. She knew better than to call and distract him while he was working. He would update her as soon as there was anything to update her with.

The sound of the front door closing made everyone in the room look up and a few seconds later Jake's eyes widened in anticipation as Connor and Danny walked through the door. Jazz's heart broke for him all over again when he saw that Isla wasn't with them.

'Didn't you find her?' Siobhan asked as tears ran down her face.

'Not yet, but we will,' Danny assured her as he walked over to Jake and gave him a brief hug.

Connor looked at the two police officers and then back at Jazz before shooting her a look that said he needed to talk to them all out of their earshot.

'Could you two give us a few moments' privacy, please?' she asked, her tone much sharper than it had been a few minutes earlier.

The two officers stared at her, aware that it wasn't a request, but no doubt having been advised by their boss to keep their ears open for any information that might either help their case or suggest that the Carters were taking matters into their own hands.

'We should probably check in with the boss anyway,' one of them said with a sigh and the other rolled their eyes, but the two of them walked out of the kitchen.

Danny took the stool beside Jake, and Connor leaned on the counter next to his wife.

'So, did you find out anything?' Jazz asked, aware they needed to talk quickly. The police would find an excuse to come back into the room in a few moments' time.

Danny swallowed hard and Connor shook his head. 'Not yet.'

'Fuck,' Jake muttered and Danny closed his eyes and bowed his head as though he was deeply ashamed.

'Luke and John have been speaking with the employees from Charlie's, but they've not come up with anything yet. That doesn't mean they're not still looking though,' Connor assured them. 'We have pulled in every single person we could to do a city-wide search. There's at least fifty people out there looking for her right now.'

'What have you two been doing?' Jake asked with a frown. 'If Luke and John are following up on the play centre.'

Connor sighed and it was Danny who answered. 'We've been looking for Milo—'

'Milo?' Jake snapped, interrupting Danny's sentence. 'Why the fuck have you been wasting time looking for that prick?'

'Because he could be involved, Jake,' Jazz answered his question. 'Isla was never supposed to have been there this morning. What if Paul was the target but...' Jazz closed her eyes as the thought of someone taking her baby made her knees almost buckle. 'But, for whatever reason, they took Isla instead.'

Siobhan started to sob again and Jake wrapped an arm around her shoulder. 'Did you find him?' he hissed.

'No,' Connor shook his head solemnly. 'Still nothing.'

'If it was him though, surely we'd have heard something? He must have had an accomplice, and you have had ears and eyes out looking everywhere for him for weeks now?' Jazz asked, no longer so sure that they were chasing the right person.

'So who the fuck took her?' Jake asked, his voice wobbling as he spoke. 'Who would...?' He shook his head, unable to finish speaking.

'We're working on it, mate. I promise you,' Connor said.

'Who have Luke and John spoken to so far?' Jazz asked as her brain ticked over with what to do next.

'They've spoken to all but one employee, and they're on their way to the last one now,' Danny replied.

'We need the list of people who were there this morning too,' Jazz said, her brows knitted into a frown as she considered how they might get it.

'Yeah, but that information is locked down tighter than Fort Knox right now,' Danny said with a sigh. 'We called all of our contacts and none of them could access it.'

'And none of the employees can access it?' Jazz asked.

'No, love. The police took it as soon as they arrived at the scene.'

'They showed it to Jake and Siobhan,' Jazz said, remembering the interview at Charlie's Play Centre. She had glanced at the list too over Jake's shoulder, but it was all just names and phone numbers. There were none that she recognised and she certainly didn't remember any of the contact telephone numbers. 'Do you remember any of the names on there?' She directed her question to Jake and Siobhan, grasping at straws now.

'No.' Jake shook his head.

'No,' Siobhan whispered.

'We'll get back out there and do whatever it takes,' Danny insisted.

'But where will you go?' Jazz asked. 'Unless we have a lead to follow, maybe you're both better here for now, and we can put our heads together and come up with a new plan?'

'We still need to find Milo,' Connor said with a sigh. 'We can't rule him out.'

'And Nudge,' Jazz whispered, aware the police were possibly right outside the door. 'We don't know if this is all connected somehow.'

'What are you all on about?' Siobhan asked. 'What does any of this have to do with my Isla? What the hell have you been doing, Jake?'

'The same stuff I always do,' he said, his features twisted in a scowl. 'The same stuff I was doing when you tricked me into marrying you.'

Siobhan flinched at the anger in his tone.

'You two turning on each other is not going to help right now,' Jazz said calmly. 'We all need to work together more than ever on this.'

'What time are my dad and Grace due back?' Connor asked, checking his watch.

'Should be landing in about half an hour,' Jazz replied.

'My mum will know what to do,' Jake said as he looked

at each of them, silently pleading with them to agree with him, because he had to believe that somebody could fix this mess.

'Yeah,' Connor and Danny agreed.

Jazz didn't reply. For the first time in her life, she wasn't sure Grace could fix this.

Chapter Twenty

G race was opening the door as soon as the car rolled to a stop on the gravel drive of their Liverpool home. They had been picked up from the airport by one of Cartel Securities' employees and he had broken every speed limit from Manchester airport to Mossley Hill to get them home as fast as possible.

'I'll get the kids, love,' Michael said as he began unbuckling Oscar's car seat.

'Thanks.' She turned briefly and smiled at him and Belle, who was asleep beside them. Then she climbed out of the car and almost ran to the door as it was opened by her daughter-in-law. Sean, Sophia and their two daughters were on the next flight home and would also be here in a few hours.

'Hi, Grace,' Jazz said, pulling her into a hug as soon as she reached her. 'It's so good to have you back.'

Grace hugged her briefly before pulling away. 'Where is Jake?'

'He's in the kitchen,' Jazz said softly as she stepped aside.

Grace ran into the kitchen and her heart almost broke as she saw her son sitting at the kitchen island with his head in his hands, looking completely broken and defeated. Danny sat beside him, Siobhan sat opposite, and Patrick and Sue were sitting at the kitchen table with Connor. There were two people she didn't recognise leaning against the kitchen counter, who she assumed were police officers.

Everyone but Jake looked up as she entered the room but he kept his head low, as though he hadn't heard her come in.

'Jake,' she said when she reached him and only then did he look up.

'Mum?' He blinked at her and suddenly all she saw was her frightened little boy whom she had sworn she would do anything to protect. How could she have let this happen to him? She wrapped her arms around him and he sagged against her. A few seconds later, the sobs started to rack his body as she held him tight. She looked across at her former daughter-in-law Siobhan, who had silent tears running down her cheeks. Grace held out her arm and beckoned the young woman to her. Siobhan came around the counter and soon Grace was holding them both as they cried together.

'We'll get her back. I promise you,' she whispered as she stroked their hair. She didn't know how she was going to do it, but she would.

When Belle and Oscar were settled in bed and Jazz had made a fresh pot of tea, the family gathered around the kitchen island. Grace had asked the police officers to give them some privacy and they had reluctantly agreed. She wondered if it was usual for them to be there the entire time, but she would check it out with Leigh. She took a deep breath as she tried to hold herself together. The time for falling apart would come later. But for now, Grace Carter was back and she would get the job done.

'So, who's going to bring me up to speed?' she asked, directing her question to Jazz and Connor because Jake and Siobhan still appeared, understandably, somewhat dazed and confused.

'You can't get out of Charlie's Play Centre unless the staff open the door. They are absolutely certain that no child would ever be allowed to leave without an adult. I know their CCTV is lax but I've been there and the staff on the front desk are hot on that front.'

'She would never have walked out of there on her own,' Grace said, her brows knitted together as she processed the information being given to her. Unlike her father, Isla was a stickler for following rules. Perhaps to her detriment. If an adult told her to do something, she generally did it. There was no way she would have left Charlie's Play Centre unless someone told her to.

'No,' Jazz agreed. 'So what we, and the police, believe is

that Isla must have been taken by someone who was at the soft play centre this morning.'

'And how many people would that be?'

'About two hundred in all. And a dozen members of staff if we're not ruling them out.'

'And we know who these people are?' Grace asked.

'We know the staff. That was easy enough to get hold of. John and Luke have spoken with every one of them and are convinced they had nothing to do with it. Mostly just kids working there, to be honest. Nothing dodgy about any of them as far as we can see. The police have the list of customers' names. We're working on getting that list ourselves but we're not having much luck right now,' Connor replied. 'Our contacts in the force tell us they're keeping it locked down so that we don't get our hands on it. They've all been told if it does get out, there will be a full inquiry and whoever was involved will lose their job and serve jail time. Apparently the Chief Constable is terrified that we're gonna go round and beat the shit out of every person on it or something.'

Grace nodded her understanding. She could see how that would be a worry, but still it didn't help their cause right now. She wasn't used to not being able to get information when they needed it.

'We have some names from our own enquiries, but we're missing most of them and their contact details.'

'And you've tried all of our police contacts? Even the senior ones?' Grace asked.

'Yep,' Jazz replied. 'It's being kept closely guarded within the Major Incident Team. I suggested we could look at it and see if we could cross-reference any telephone numbers even if we didn't recognise a name, but they said we'd significantly jeopardise the investigation if we start interrogating witnesses. Their team is interviewing everyone on the list.'

'Fuck,' Michael muttered beside her. 'We need to interview them ourselves.'

'Yeah,' Connor agreed. 'Luke and John are already making a start on the names we have, but the boys in blue are onto them and keep trying to warn them off. That's why we got our very own personal officers assigned here. Of course they say it's protocol in case we get any contact from the kidnappers.'

'And has there been any contact? From anyone?'

'No,' Jake replied, as though he was suddenly back in the room.

'We've got our entire available workforce out there looking for Isla and asking questions, Grace, but so far we've got nothing,' Danny said solemnly.

Grace rubbed her temples as she tried to think of what to do next. The fact that the police were involved tied their hands significantly, but there was nothing she wouldn't do and no law she wouldn't break to bring Isla home safely.

'And there's no CCTV that can help?' she asked.

'No,' Sue spoke for the first time. 'They don't have any near the doorway.'

'But they do have some of Isla playing with a bunch of kids, so the police are trying to identify the children and their parents.'

'Police are checking CCTV of some of the shops nearby but because Charlie's entrance is tucked away around the side, there's nothing of their car park, although plenty of the hundreds of cars that went in and out of the retail estate that morning,' Connor replied.

'I suppose we don't have the list of cars either?'

'Nope. But we're working on that too,' Connor said.

'Where are John and Luke right now?' she asked.

'Making the last house call of the night,' Danny said as he checked his watch. 'They'll be back here soon.'

Grace nodded. 'Good.'

'What do we do now, Mum?' Jake asked her and she wished more than anything in the world that she had a better answer to his question than the one she was about to give. 'We get those lists, son. Who owns Charlie's Play Centre?'

'Some fella who lives in Wigan,' Connor replied. 'Brendan Dryhurst. One of our lads spoke to him. He never goes near the place really. Hasn't been there in over a week and his staff all back that up. Has a nursing home in Birkenhead that he owns but doesn't give a shit about too. Just takes the profits and treats his staff like crap by all accounts.'

'So he has a manager run the play centre?'

'Yeah,' Danny answered. 'Luke spoke to her earlier. She

lives in Huyton. Single mum with two little kids of her own. He didn't get anything suspicious from her.'

Grace frowned as she thought about the next step and which of those two people she would prefer to be escorted from their house at almost midnight. There was only one obvious answer.

'Well, Mr Dryhurst might not be able to get us this week's list of customers, but he can certainly get his hands on the lists from every other Saturday. If this was a planned attack then surely whoever did this must be a regular, right?'

'Of course,' Jazz agreed. 'Why didn't we think of that?'

'I guess I'll call Luke and John and ask them to make one more house call to Brendan then?' Connor said, seemingly thankful for something to do.

'I can go,' Danny offered.

'The police might still be at the soft play centre. It's still a crime scene, and if the records are still there and Brendan has to be taken there to pick them up, then they're more likely to recognise you than Luke if you were there earlier.'

'I suppose,' Danny agreed reluctantly.

'If the perpetrator was smart they'd have used an alias, but at least we can identify regular customers. Even that's a start right now. In the meantime, we still need to work on getting the names from today too,' Grace added.

'Yes we do,' Jazz agreed. 'Any idea how?'

'Leave it with me,' Grace said, thinking of the one favour she could still call in. Slipping away from her family, she dialled the number. It went to voicemail, as she'd suspected it would.

She left a message asking him to call her back as soon as possible, hoping that he'd do it sooner rather than later.

Chapter Twenty-One

Luke Sullivan sat back against the heated leather seat as John Brennan drove them down the M58 towards Wigan.

'Apparently this fella's house is massive,' John said as he peered through the windscreen. 'Gates and everything.'

'Well, this beast will be able to drive right through them if he doesn't open them up, John,' Luke suggested.

'Fuck off!' John snapped. He'd driven a BMW X5 for as long as Luke had known him and had recently upgraded to a new one.

Luke laughed softly. 'I'm sure we can think of another way to get through them.'

'If he's in. It's Saturday night and all,' John said.

'Well, I fucking hope he is, mate, because I feel like shit that we've been at this all day and night and still have fuck all, to be honest.'

'Me too,' John said with a sigh. 'I hope she's okay, Luke.'

'Yeah,' Luke agreed. He hadn't seen Jake since Isla was taken, but he'd kept in regular contact with Danny. He didn't know what he was even going to say when he saw him. What was the right thing to say in such situations? He couldn't even imagine what Jake was going through. It was hard enough for him to focus, given what had happened, and Isla wasn't even his child. The least he could do was get the information they needed from Brendan Dryhurst.

It was only ten minutes later when John pulled his car up outside the house belonging to the owner of Charlie's Play Centre. He stopped at the gate and pressed the intercom. Luke wondered if anyone would answer, given that it was almost midnight, but there were lights on downstairs so he figured that was a good sign.

'Who is it?' a voice answered.

'Detectives Grosvenor and King,' John replied without missing a beat. 'We're here about the little girl who went missing from your establishment today.'

'Of course,' came the reply and then the electronic gates started to open.

'That was easy,' Luke said.

'No camera,' John said, pointing to the intercom. 'Not like he could ask to see any ID.'

Luke nodded his appreciation of John's quick thinking as he drove the car up the small drive and came to a stop. The two men jumped out of the car and walked to the front door, which was already being opened by a tall man with glasses and a grey beard.

John and Luke jogged up the couple of steps and suddenly Brendan Dryhurst's face dropped. These two looked nothing like police detectives.

'Can I s-see your ID?' he stammered.

John pushed through the door, causing Brendan to stagger backwards and almost fall flat on his arse. 'Yeah, we don't have any of that,' he snapped as he looked around the hallway.

Luke popped his head into the room nearby where the sound of the television was coming from. 'No one in here,' he said. They'd been informed that Brendan lived alone but they still wanted to check. They didn't need the police getting called while they were interrogating him – if he decided to be uncooperative, then things could get messy.

'Wh-who are you?' Brendan asked as he scooted backwards on the floor until he was pressed against the stairwell.

'Well, I suppose that all depends on how helpful you are, Brendan,' Luke said as he walked toward him.

'What do you want?' he whispered, his face turning paler by the second.

Luke glanced at John. Brendan already looked like he was about to pass out and he suspected they weren't going to get much resistance from him, which he was grateful for.

'The records from Charlie's Play Centre. I want the lists of the people who visited there every Saturday for the past three months.'

'Are you looking for that little girl?' he asked. 'Are you trying to find her?'

'The lists, Brendan,' Luke snarled.

He blinked at the two of them.

'Where are they?' John demanded.

'H-here, in my office,' Brendan said, wiping the sweat from his brow.

'Then go get them like a good boy,' Luke suggested, grateful that they were here and they wouldn't have to fuck about trying to get into the soft play centre, which would still be designated a crime scene.

Brendan nodded vigorously, pushing himself up and scurrying along the hallway with Luke and John close behind him. The office had a keycode and he entered it quickly before stepping inside and turning on the light. Luke followed him in while John waited outside. It was a neat and tidy space and Luke noticed the security camera on the ceiling in the corner of the room.

'Is that thing recording?' he asked.

'Yes.' Brendan swallowed. 'It's motion activated.'

Luke nodded. He kept his head down but the camera didn't particularly bother him. He wasn't doing anything illegal. Brendan was handing the information over of his own free will. They hadn't even had to threaten him.

Luke watched as the older man rifled through some filing cabinets before pulling out a number of sheets of paper. He had to give it to him, he kept a good filing system.

'Here are the last three months,' Brendan said, holding out the pieces of paper.

Luke took them and glanced through them, noting that everything seemed to be there that he'd asked for. 'You got something for me to put these in?'

'Y-yes,' Brendan stammered as he picked up a brown A4 envelope.

Luke took it from him and placed the contents inside. 'Thank you for your co-operation, Mr Dryhurst. Should you feel the need to discuss this visit with anyone else, my colleague and I will be in touch,' he said, his eyes narrowed as he stared at the other man.

Brendan nodded his understanding and Luke was thankful for his compliance. He'd never had a job go so smoothly before.

'Let's go, big fella,' he said to John as he walked out of the office. A few moments later, the two of them were safely ensconced in John's X5 and heading back to Liverpool.

'That was too fucking easy, right?' John said with a dark laugh as he drove them home.

'Yeah, but I don't think Brendan has ever thrown a punch in his life,' Luke replied with a shrug. 'Not like we took anything of value to him, is it?'

'Suppose not,' John agreed.

'Let's just hope they're valuable to us though, eh?'

'Yes, let's fucking hope so.'

Chapter Twenty-Two

I t was after 1 a.m. by the time John Brennan and Luke Sullivan arrived at Grace's house. After exchanging greetings, Grace ushered them out into the garden with Michael, Connor, Danny and Jazz so they could talk out of the earshot of the police, leaving Jake and Siobhan in the kitchen.

'Did you get what you needed from Dryhurst?' Grace asked as they all sat on the patio furniture at the far end of the large garden.

'Yes,' Luke said, pulling an A4 envelope out from inside his coat. 'He only keeps paper records, but he keeps most of them at his home office. He picked these up on his last visit a week and a half ago, so they have the last three months of Saturday customers right there.'

'Nice work,' Grace said with a smile. 'We can start checking them as soon as we get back inside.'

'Did you find out anything else from him or his staff?' Michael asked.

'Nothing at all,' Luke sighed and shook his head. 'Dryhurst rarely goes to the place, so he was useless beyond providing those records. But his staff team seemed genuinely upset and really affected by Isla going missing. They all bent over backwards to help us. They'd already been interviewed by the police, but they were all more than willing to answer our questions too.'

'Did you get the names of any customers?' Michael asked.

'About half a dozen regulars but no contact details,' John replied. 'The only people with those details right now are the police but they're playing their cards very close to their chests on this one.'

'I'll get you the names,' Grace assured them. 'So there was nothing else helpful at all?' she asked again.

'No, but me and John were talking,' Luke replied. 'I mean, Isla never went to the soft play place before, right? Pat and Sue used to take Paul every Saturday, but they'd never taken Isla?'

'No,' Connor replied.

'So, how did anyone know Isla was going to be there?'

'Well, they couldn't have,' Michael said, rubbing a hand over his beard as he sat back in his chair.

'So maybe they didn't target Isla because of who she is?' Luke offered. 'Maybe they were just looking for any child?' He whispered the last words because the reasons why someone might be looking for a child didn't bear thinking about.

'Sick fucks!' Michael snarled as though he was reading his mind.

'We're looking into the possibility that it could be Milo Savage,' Connor said.

'The fella who tried to take Jazz and have you set up for murder?' Michael frowned.

'Yeah,' Jazz replied. 'Like Luke said, it was Paul who went there every week and not Isla.'

'Hmm,' Grace murmured as she thought about anyone else who would have targeted her granddaughter. They had all made many enemies over the years.

'Any luck finding him yet?' Michael asked.

'No,' Connor said with a heavy sigh.

'We need that list and fast, Grace,' John added. 'It's the best chance we have.'

'I'm working on it, but in the meantime is there any chance you could help with that, big man?' she asked him.

'Of course I'll ask her, Grace, but Leigh isn't on this case and she doesn't have easy access to it. She could lose her job.'

'I could lose my granddaughter,' she replied and he nodded.

'I'll ask her when I get home.'

'Thank you,' she said with a smile.

'There's something else you need to know about, Grace,' Connor said, clearing his throat. The way that Jazz, Luke and John looked at him made Grace's blood freeze in her veins. 'Jake was going to tell you today, but then with everything else, it kind of...' Connor trailed off and Jazz squeezed his hand reassuringly.

'What is it?' Grace asked as both she and Michael sat forward in their chairs.

'Nudge Richards was murdered last night,' Connor said quietly, conscious that there were two police officers in his kitchen, even though they were too far away to hear.

'What?' Grace gasped, her hand flying to her mouth as she too remembered their guests would be watching and trying to listen.

'By who?' Michael asked, as he took hold of Grace's free hand in his and laced his fingers through hers. Grace held his hand tightly, his firm, warm grip giving her some comfort.

'We don't know, Dad. I went there to deal with another problem and I found him with his throat cut. We were going to start looking into it today, but then Isla went missing and...' He shook his head.

'Oh my God. Poor Nudge,' Grace whispered as a tear rolled down her cheek. 'Who would do that?'

'Nudge knew more dodgy people than the rest of us put together, love,' Michael reminded her.

'I know, but...' Grace stopped talking as she thought about her friend. So terrifying to look at yet so loyal and kind-hearted deep down.

'What did you do with him?' Michael asked his son.

'We had to bury him,' Connor whispered. 'We couldn't

chance the bizzies declaring his yard a murder scene and crawling all over it.'

'Of course not. You did the right thing,' Michael assured him.

'We're just going to put the word out that he retired. He doesn't own the yard anyway, right?'

'No. It's ours,' Grace whispered.

'We buried him properly, Grace. Me and Jake. We said some nice words and that,' Connor said apologetically.

Grace reached across the table and placed her hand over Connor's. 'Thank you.'

They sat in silence for a few moments and it felt fitting as they thought about their former friend and associate. 'Do you think what happened to Nudge had anything to do with someone taking Isla?' Michael eventually asked.

'Never say no, but what would be the connection? Or the endgame?' Grace asked.

'Taking you lot out,' John suggested. 'Let's face it, if someone other than us had found Nudge, then that would have been a murder scene. And who knows what they might have found there that could have brought any number of you down?'

'You think we're that stupid that we'd leave evidence behind, John?' Michael snapped.

'No, but even the most careful of people can leave a trace of something,' John reminded him. 'And there have been more bodies disposed of in that yard than at Anfield Crematorium.'

'I wasn't even supposed to be there last night. It was a last-minute thing. Maybe John has a point?' Connor said.

'That would be a motive for killing Nudge,' Grace admitted. 'But taking Isla?'

'Which brings us back to Milo Savage,' Michael said. 'If this is about bringing this family down – well, taking one of our kids is the worst thing anyone could do, isn't it?'

'I did think of him as soon as this happened,' Jazz said with a frown. 'And maybe he was responsible for Nudge if it was about getting us nicked. I mean, he's tried that before. But who would have helped him? Because he has no friends in Liverpool, or anywhere else, it seems.'

'Well, he must have a friend somewhere because he seems to have disappeared off the face of the earth.'

'Maybe he has? Probably has plenty of enemies. You think someone beat you to it?' John asked.

'Fuck knows,' Connor said with a deep sigh. 'But we've been looking for him for weeks and no fucker knows where he is.'

'So we need to find him too,' Grace replied. 'But for now, let's work on getting these names.'

At that, John stood up. 'I'll go ask my girlfriend if she can do anything about that then, eh?' he said.

'Thank you, John,' Grace replied as she stood too and gave him a hug. 'I appreciate it.'

Chapter Twenty-Three

G race saw the unknown number flashing on her mobile phone and excused herself from the kitchen to answer it.

'Grace Carter?' the voice on the other end asked.

'Andy. How long has it been?' she replied.

'Not long enough,' he replied with a sarcastic laugh. 'But then forever wouldn't be long enough when it comes to you.'

'Oh, you flatter me.'

'Huh,' he snorted. 'So, what is it?'

'I need some information.'

'Don't we all.'

'I'm serious. My granddaughter has been kidnapped.'

'Oh,' he said, suddenly his tone more serious. Not only because of the gravity of the situation, but also because he now knew she was about to ask him to put his entire career on the line.

Andy Dixon had been the young and upcoming Sergeant who had put her ex-husband, as well as half of the Liverpool underworld, away for long stretches over twenty years earlier. He had acted on information that Grace provided, and the case had made his career, leading him to his current position, which was so high up in the National Crime Agency that Grace didn't even know what his title was.

That was how they'd met, at least, but that wasn't why he owed her a debt.

'MIT are handling the case and they have a list of witnesses that I can't get access to. But I need those names, Andy. She's been missing for almost fourteen hours now.'

'Can't you use your usual contacts?'

'This is my son's daughter. You know who he is. They're keeping this list locked down to a select few people.'

'If I access this, one of those people could lose their job.'

'If you don't, my granddaughter could lose her life,' she snapped. 'And if that happens…'

'Okay,' he replied with a sigh. She didn't need to finish that sentence. 'God, I miss you.'

'Two minutes ago you told me that forever wouldn't be long enough, so which is it?'

'Can't it be both?'

'I suppose.'

'You miss me?'

'Not anymore,' she told him honestly.

'Ouch.' He laughed softly.

'A lot has changed in twenty-two years, Andy.'

'Not everything though, it seems. You always know how to get hold of me even when I'm off-grid.'

'You tell me every time you change your number. Worried in case I call your office looking for you?'

'Maybe. And because I owe you my life, Grace Sumner, and no amount of time will change that.'

'It's Carter now, as you well know.'

'Hmm.'

'I miss him though,' Grace admitted. 'Every single day.'

'Me too,' Andy said quietly. 'So you want this list?'

'Yes. How quickly can you get it for me?'

'As soon as possible. Twenty-four hours, max.'

'I don't have that long,' she said, her brows knitted in a frown.

'I will do everything I can to get it to you sooner.'

'Thank you.'

Grace ended the call and slipped her phone into the pocket of her jeans as she thought about her old friends.

During Nathan's trial, Andy had fallen in love with her best friend, Marcus. They had been perfect for each other. With Nathan in prison and her on/off relationship with Ben going through an off patch, she had been their third wheel. They had been the greatest of friends for over a year. But Andy had refused to tell anyone he was gay, believing it would jeopardise his career. And although Marcus had accepted it for a time, the final straw had been when some of Andy's colleagues had called Marcus some horrible, homophobic names and he'd just stood by and let them. It had been the end of their relationship.

Both of them had been broken-hearted, but Marcus knew his worth too well. He knew he deserved more than a man who wasn't willing to stand up for him.

Marcus moved on, although he never quite fell as hard for anyone ever again. Andy took their break-up badly and, despite Marcus being her closest friend, it was Grace he turned to. Grace he called the night he took too many pills. Grace who took him to the hospital and held his hand while he had his stomach pumped. Grace who lied to his colleagues and told them she was his girlfriend, when he'd seen a couple of them in the A&E department that same night. Grace who kept his secret and never told a soul about what he'd done. Grace who reminded him that he had a whole life ahead of him. He moved to Manchester and started afresh, but, as far as she knew, he'd never settled down with anyone.

When Marcus had been murdered a few years earlier, Andy hadn't even come to his funeral, but Grace knew that every single day he lived with the sadness and regret of not following his heart. She hated to use his pain for her own ends, but she had no choice when it came to her family.

Chapter Twenty-Four

L eigh was sitting up in bed when John got home.

'Late again,' she said with a smile.

'I'm lucky I got to come home at all,' he said with a heavy sigh as he sat on the edge of the bed and started to pull off his boots.

'How are they all over there?'

'As you'd expect, I suppose. Everyone is at Grace and Michael's house and, I don't know, it kind of feels like the world is standing still in there, you know? And then you step outside the door and it starts turning again.'

'Have they still heard nothing?' she said as she put her book on the bedside table.

'Nope. It might not even be a ransom situation, Leigh. It could just be some bastard looking for a kid.'

He pulled off his clothes, climbed into bed beside her and drew her into his arms. 'Jake is just walking around like a zombie, and poor Siobhan, I swear my heart breaks every time I look at her.'

'I can't even imagine what they're going through,' Leigh said.

'They could really use that list of names from the soft play centre.'

'I told you I can't access it, John. They're keeping it closed down. This case is so high-profile that it has its own level of clearance. My superiors aren't stupid enough to believe that Jake and Connor don't have at least some of my colleagues in their pockets. They won't risk this investigation by allowing those names to fall into your employers' hands. Only a few select people have the whole list. Even Grosvenor's own team only have part of it each. This case is being handled with the highest level of security.'

'There's no way you could get it?'

She drew back and frowned at him. 'No. And any attempt would cost me my job.'

'I know, but it's a little kid, Leigh.'

'I know that too, John, but Grosvenor's team are doing everything they can, and I really don't think that sending the Carters' mindless thugs to interrogate the key witnesses is going to help matters. Let the police handle it.'

'It's hard to sit back and do nothing, Leigh. Especially when I see the effect it's having. Especially when so far the police have come up with jack shit.'

'Give them time, John. They are doing everything they can. I promise.'

'Time might not be a luxury Isla has,' he reminded her. 'You know that the first twenty-four hours in a missing person's case is the most crucial, Leigh?'

She laid her head back down, nestling against his chest. 'I promise I will help any way I can, but I don't have the clearance to access those names.'

'Okay. I'll tell Grace I asked you, but don't be surprised if she asks you herself anyway.'

'Are you always going to be loyal to Grace Carter?' she whispered.

'What can I say? I'm a loyal kind of guy,' he said with a faint laugh.

'John, I'm being serious.' She nudged him in the ribs.

'Doesn't mean I can't be loyal to you too, Leigh. She asked me to do something and I agreed to do it because she's my friend. I was completely honest with you about it. You told me you can't do it and I respect that. What more do you want from me?'

'I just want to know that you'll always have my back the way you have hers, that's all.'

He grabbed her chin with his hand and turned her face up to his. 'I have always got your back, Detective.'

She rolled her eyes and he responded by rolling her onto her back and pinning her hands beside her head. 'I've always got your front too,' he grinned at her, making her laugh before he sealed her lips with his and tried to forget about the horrible day he'd had.

Leigh was in the staff room boiling the kettle for her third coffee of the morning when DI Grosvenor walked in and closed the door behind him.

'Everything okay, Kev?' she asked.

'Not really. We've still got nothing on the missing girl,' he said with a sigh. 'I'm just off to the house now to meet with the family again, which is why I wanted a quick word.'

'Oh?' She frowned.

'You know Grace and Michael Carter are back?'

'I assumed they would be,' she replied as she stirred her coffee.

'You've had dealings with them before, right?'

'Yeah?' Her frown deepened as she wondered where he could possibly be going with this.

'Any tips for handling them? I mean, what are they like? I've heard rumours about Michael Carter that can't possibly be true, but still.' He shuddered.

'Are you scared, Kev?' She started to laugh.

'No. Let's just say I'm being prudently cautious.'

'Well, it's not Michael Carter you have to worry about. Grace Carter is the one in charge. Win her over and you'll be golden.'

'You think?'

'Yep, and remember we're all on the same side on this one, right?'

'Yeah. I still feel like I'm walking into the fucking lion's den.'

'Behave yourself.' She laughed harder. 'I'm sure Danny

won't hold a grudge for you locking him up for a few weeks for nothing.'

'Thanks, Leigh. Now I feel a whole lot better,' he snapped.

'Hey, have you considered whether this whole thing would be handled a lot faster if you just gave the Carters the list of suspects?'

'Leigh!' He frowned at her. 'What the fuck?'

'It's just a question, Kev. It's not like I'd actually ever do it.'

'I think it would end up with every witness on the list ending up in A&E, so no, I haven't considered handing our only line of inquiry over to a group of violent gangsters, Leigh, no.'

'I doubt they would put everyone in A&E,' Leigh said confidently, aware that John had already spoken to a number of them himself and with no casualties.

'You sound like you're on their side.' He arched an eyebrow at her.

'I suppose on this I am. I mean, nobody wants that little girl hurt, do they?'

'No. But I don't want anyone else hurt either,' he reminded her.

'Of course. I was just playing devil's advocate,' she said with a shrug, trying to appear as nonchalant as she could. 'Now that Grace is back in Liverpool, I'm sure there will be a resolution one way or another.'

'Sometimes I get the impression you admire Grace Carter,' DI Grosvenor said as he leaned against the counter and stared at her. It sounded like an accusation but Leigh wasn't fazed by it. As good as he was at his job, she didn't believe he was completely straight – and his conduct in the recent murder investigation had reinforced her suspicion.

'I do admire her. She's a woman who rules a man's world and she does it without causing absolute carnage in her wake.'

'I have a feeling some people might disagree with you,' he sneered.

'The kind of people Grace Carter makes enemies of are not the kind of people I lose much sleep over, Kev. She protects her family and the people she cares about. She may not do it the same way we would, but…'

'Well, I doubt we'll ever agree on that score,' he said dismissively.

'We'll see,' she said with a smile.

'What's that supposed to mean?' He frowned again.

'Go meet her and then tell me you don't admire her,' Leigh challenged him.

Grosvenor straightened his tie. 'Then I suppose we'll see,' he said with a wry smile before he walked out of the room.

As soon as Leigh was in the privacy of her own car a few moments later, she made the call.

'Hi, Leigh,' Grace Carter said when she picked up.

'Hi, Grace. Look, I'm sorry I couldn't help with the list,

but the guy who has access to it is on his way to Connor's house now. DI Grosvenor.'

'Yes. Jazz mentioned he was the one in charge. What are you suggesting, Leigh?'

'I don't know, to be honest. He's not going to give you those names, and please don't tie him up and try and torture them out of him,' she said, only half joking. 'But just be nice to him, okay? Show him the Grace Carter who charms psychopaths for a living, and just maybe he'll let something useful slip. I mean, he's like most men, really, stroke his ego and...'

'I understand. I'll tell the boys to be on their best behaviour too. Thank you, Leigh.'

'You're welcome. I hope she's found soon, Grace. I really do.'

Chapter Twenty-Five

DI Grosvenor stood on the doorstep of Grace and Michael Carter's house waiting for the door to be answered. He took a quick glance around him, noting the gated walls, the perfectly manicured garden and the array of expensive cars in the driveway. And they said crime didn't pay. Seems like this lot hadn't got the memo. He shook his head in exasperation.

A few seconds later, the door opened and Jasmine Carter's face appeared. She opened the door wide. 'Please, come on in,' she said with a faint smile. 'Everyone is in the kitchen.'

DI Grosvenor nodded politely before he followed her along the hallway and into the kitchen where almost the entire family were gathered. He noticed Michael and Sean Carter sitting together at the dining table. He'd never had any personal dealings with them, but everyone in

Merseyside Police knew their faces. They had been active for over twenty-five years and at the top of the tree for most of that time. They'd both served a couple of stretches for drug supply in the past, but since they'd got out years earlier, they had been squeaky clean – at least on the surface, but he knew that men like that never really changed. They just got smarter and better at covering their tracks. He had an idea that the woman walking in from the garden with a baby in her arms had something to do with that. The infamous Grace Carter. He'd never met her personally either, but her reputation preceded her.

He had met most of the rest of the family at the crime scene the previous day and he offered them a nod of greeting as he was ushered to a chair by Jasmine.

'You must be Detective Inspector Grosvenor,' Grace said as she approached him.

'Here, let me take him,' Jasmine said as she took the baby from her mother-in-law's arms.

'Go to your mummy,' the older woman said, planting a soft kiss on the baby's head. Then she gave DI Grosvenor her full attention. Extending her hand to him, she said, 'DI Grosvenor? I'm Grace Carter.'

She looked him squarely in the eyes as she spoke and he stared into her brown eyes, which crinkled when she smiled. He gripped her hand in his, shaking it and noting the softness of her skin as her fingers closed over his. He had to admit, there was something captivating about her. When she gave you her undivided attention she made you feel like you were the only person in the room.

'Do you have any updates for us, Detective?' she asked and he realised he was staring at her. Her husband suddenly appeared at her side and the hairs on the back of Kevin's neck stood on end.

'Please, call me Kevin,' he said with a wave of his hand.

'Have you found our little girl yet, Kevin?' a voice came from behind him and he swivelled in his chair to see Siobhan, the missing girl's mother, her eyes deep red and her face pale. He had four children himself – three sons and a daughter – and he couldn't even comprehend the terror and anxiety that she must be feeling right now. Despite who they were, he was determined to bring their child home. It didn't help matters that they were making enquiries of their own, though he and his team had asked them repeatedly not to, but he supposed that if he were in their shoes he might do the same.

'We're pursuing every line of inquiry we have. We're working our way through every single person who was at the play centre yesterday. We will find who took her,' he assured her, but her eyes glazed over and she went to sit beside Jake Conlon at the kitchen island. He put a protective arm around her and she all but crumpled against him.

'Do you have any idea where she is?' Grace asked him.

'Not yet,' he admitted. 'But we are—'

'Pursuing every line of inquiry,' Jake interrupted him and Kevin nodded. He had repeated that line at least a dozen times himself in the last twenty hours, but what else was he supposed to say? *At this present moment, we have no idea who took your daughter and why.*

He had assumed that there would be a ransom demand, or possibly it was some kind of revenge attack, but if that were the case he would have expected contact from the kidnappers by now. Quite a few people from Charlie's Play Centre remembered little Isla. They saw her in the ball pool and on the trampolines, and in the football enclosure. She'd chatted to a few of the children they'd already spoken to, but no one remembered her leaving with anyone. Nobody recalled the moment when she was suddenly not there. Kevin had even had his team comb through every part of the centre again, in case she had got herself stuck somewhere, or hidden in some dark space as part of a game, but the girl was nowhere on the premises. He was confident they would find her. His team were interviewing everyone who was present yesterday. He only hoped they would find her in time.

'We will find out who took your daughter,' he repeated.

'Yeah, right,' Jake snarled.

'If you gave us that list of names you're working through, we would find her in no time,' Michael Carter said.

'You know I can't do that,' Kevin replied with a sigh. 'Please just let my team do their jobs.'

'Of course, Kevin,' Grace interrupted as she placed a hand on his arm. 'Can we get you a cup of tea while you update us on who you've spoken with so far and the progress your team has made?'

He blinked at her. Was she being genuine or taking the piss?

'I'll pop the kettle on, love,' the lady he recognised as Sue, the great-grandmother, said.

'Thanks, Sue,' Grace replied.

Kevin sat with his mug of tea and briefed the family on the limited progress they had made so far. He expected a tirade of questions as to why he wasn't doing more. Why he wasn't doing enough. He expected the hostility and anger that he'd experienced yesterday, but everyone in the room remained silent. It was only Grace who spoke, asking him questions and probing for more information. She would have made a good detective. But it was as though everyone else in the room was on their best behaviour while she was there, and Kevin was thankful for it. His job was hard enough without dealing with a room full of angry men too.

He took some more information too. He asked them again about any connections they might have had at the soft play centre and who might have known that Isla would be there that day. He got exactly the same answers as he'd received the day before, but sometimes people remembered details that were seemingly unimportant but ended up being incredibly significant. He knew they hadn't been contacted by whoever took the girl because they would be out there acting on it rather than sitting there talking to him – and because he'd also stationed two of his officers here permanently.

Kevin rubbed a hand over his jaw. 'Thank you all for

your time. My officers will stay here in case you get any contact, if that's okay?'

'So what do we do now? Just sit and wait?' Grace asked him.

'I know that's hard, but yes. Let us do our jobs.'

'Okay,' she replied with a nod and a reassuring smile. But he knew full well she had no intention of doing that. He could almost see the cogs turning in her brain. He briefly wondered what they could achieve if they did pool their resources, but he dismissed the idea as quickly as it arrived. That way madness lay.

'I'll be in touch as soon as I have anything to share, and in the meantime please keep us updated if you have any information that could help us. Or if the kidnappers get in touch.'

'We will, Kevin,' Grace said as she stood, ready to escort him to the door.

After a brief conversation with the two uniformed officers, DI Grosvenor followed Grace out into the hallway. As they reached the front door, she turned and looked at him, her eyes narrowed as they searched his face. 'What are the chances of you finding her?'

He swallowed hard. 'The first twenty-four hours are crucial,' he admitted, fully aware they were fast approaching the twenty-first hour since Isla had disappeared. 'But I promise you that Isla is our top priority right now. I'll be back with the press officer in the next couple of hours and we'll talk through our next options.'

'You mean Jake and Siobhan going on telly and begging for someone to bring their baby back?'

'That's one option,' he admitted.

'You know that I could get through that list of yours by the end of the day?' she challenged him.

'That is not the way to handle this, Grace,' he replied, frowning at her.

'Well, I suppose we'll agree to disagree,' she said as she opened the door. As she did, a florist's van was pulling into the drive. She and Kevin watched as a woman climbed out with a huge bunch of flowers. They were white lilies. Grace shuddered. They had once been her favourite flowers, but now they only reminded her of her ex-husband, Nathan, and how he used to buy them for her on the many occasions he'd done something horrible.

Grace frowned. Who the hell would be sending flowers?

She glanced at Kevin, who was frowning too.

'Expecting flowers?' he asked her.

'Yes. I always like to have fresh flowers around the place,' she lied.

'Really? You had time to order yourself some flowers yesterday?' He was scowling now.

'No. My husband ordered them for me. He likes to do practical things to keep his mind occupied.'

'Hmm,' Kevin said as he watched the florist walking up

the path. 'Maybe I'll just stay and check out if there is a message. Just in case.'

'Be my guest,' Grace replied, hiding her annoyance like a seasoned pro.

'Grace Carter?' the florist asked as she approached them, blowing a strand of blonde hair from her face.

'Yes,' she said with a smile as she took the flowers. 'Thank you.'

'May I?' Kevin said as he plucked the card from the stalk in the middle of the bunch.

'Show me your list and I'll let you read my card,' Grace said as she snatched it from him.

'Mrs Carter, please don't make me arrest you for hindering a police investigation, because I will.'

'I'd like to see you try,' she challenged him, but she handed the card back to him. 'I hope you're not going to blush if my husband has had something filthy written on that card, Detective.'

That made him falter for a second, but then he tore the envelope open. 'Not from your husband at all,' he said as he held it up for her to read.

'Nope,' she said with a forced smile as the blood turned to ice in her veins. 'From our dog-sitter. He must have heard about what happened.'

'Your dog-sitter sends you flowers?'

'Looks like.'

'Right,' he replied with a slight frown. It had been the first thing to come into her head. They didn't even have a dog-sitter. Their niece Steph had been looking after their dog Bruce while they were in Spain.

'I need to get these in some water. I look forward to seeing you later,' Grace said, ushering him off the doorstep. 'Hopefully you'll have some good news for us by then?'

'I hope so.'

Grace watched until he climbed into his car and pulled out of the driveway. She and the rest of the family had been up most of the night scouring the lists that Luke and John had retrieved from Brendan Dryhurst and had managed to put together a list of people who had visited Charlie's Play Centre more than once in the past three months. But it was a long list and they had only just started working their way through it. Now, though, she wondered if they would need it at all.

As soon as Grosvenor's car was out of sight, she walked back into the house and headed straight to the kitchen carrying the flowers. She placed them on the kitchen counter and then turned to the two uniformed officers. 'I'd like you to leave my house now, please.'

They blinked at her. 'We can't.'

'Yes, you can. I've allowed you to stay here because you assured me it was the best thing to do to ensure my granddaughter's return, but actually there is nothing you can do here that you can't do elsewhere. You have all of our numbers.'

'But, we—' one of them started to say.

'I believe my wife just asked you to leave,' Michael

interrupted him. 'My family and I are going through a lot. Can you please allow us some privacy for a while. I know your boss will be back with a press team later, but until then we'd just like to be left alone.'

The two constables mumbled something unintelligible to each other and Grace sighed deeply. 'Leave my house. Now,' she shouted.

'Siobhan, Jake.' The female officer looked past Grace to the distraught parents. 'Would you like us to stay?'

'I never wanted you here in the first place,' Jake snapped while Siobhan simply shook her head as she clung to her ex-husband.

'Just for a few hours,' Grace said with a smile. They were on to her but she didn't care. She needed some privacy and she needed it now.

'Okay, but please call us if anything happens,' the female officer said.

'Of course we will,' Grace lied.

'I'll see you both out,' Michael said as he escorted the officers out of the kitchen. While he was gone, everyone looked at Grace, waiting for her to bring them up to speed.

'Who the fuck are the flowers from?' Michael asked as he walked back into the room.

'From whoever took Isla,' Grace replied.

'What?' Jake pushed his chair back and walked over to her. She handed him the card and he scanned the words written on it:

To Grace. For everything you've ever done for me. Lilies are your favourite, right?

Love

Eddie

'I don't get it, Mum,' said Jake, shaking his head.

'Lilies are the traditional flowers for grief,' Siobhan whispered and Jazz put an arm around her shoulders.

'White roses are your favourite flowers,' Michael added.

'They didn't used to be, though. It used to be lilies, a long time ago, anyway.'

Everyone in the room was frowning at Grace now or staring at her like she had two heads.

'When I was married to your dad,' she said to Jake, 'I loved lilies, but he used to buy them for me when he'd done something really awful. Now I hate them,' she said with a shudder.

'So who the fuck is Eddie?' Luke asked.

'Eddie Redman,' Grace replied.

'Why is that name familiar to me?' Michael frowned at her.

'Because you killed him.'

'Eddie!' Jake snarled as the penny dropped.

'Yes,' Grace replied. Eddie had been Jake's half-brother. Their father, Nathan, had disowned Eddie at birth but it still didn't stop him seeking revenge for Nathan's murder. That was why a few years earlier, he had kidnapped Grace and intended to kill her. Michael and Sean had found her in time and afterwards, Michael had exacted his bloody revenge on the man who had dared to put his hands on the woman he loved.

'But he's dead,' Siobhan whispered.

'Yes, but his mum isn't,' Grace replied. 'This is personal. And what better way to get back at me and Jake than to take someone we love?'

At this, Siobhan began sobbing and Jake rushed to her side and put a comforting arm around her.

'I don't think she would hurt her, Siobhan,' Grace said as she felt the weight of guilt almost crushing her. This was all her fault. Not because they had killed Eddie – that evil bastard had deserved it – but because she should have dealt with Sandra too.

Sandra Redman had been an eighteen-year-old barmaid at Grace's pub, The Rose and Crown, over twenty years ago, when she had come to the attention of Nathan Conlon. Of course she had, with her blonde pigtails and her long legs and tiny black skirt. They all came to his attention. Grace hadn't been much older herself at the time, and, pregnant with Jake, she'd had no idea of her husband's philandering ways – still clinging onto the belief that he was a good man who loved her. It was only years later that she learned that a one-night stand between the two of them had resulted in a son not that much younger than Jake – Eddie.

By that time, the fact that her rotten ex-husband had fathered another child came as no surprise to her at all. Even learning that he'd paid Sandra off and threatened to kill her if she ever revealed her son's true father hadn't shocked her. That was the kind of man he was. Causing misery and destruction wherever he went and thinking of the effect on nobody but himself. Against the odds, Grace and Sandra had even become good friends, and they had both kept the secret of Eddie's parentage from the rest of the world – knowing that it would only cause further misery if people were to discover the truth. That was why Grace was shocked to discover that, for reasons unknown to anyone but herself, Sandra told Eddie when he was twenty who his father really was. Nathan was dead by this point – murdered by Grace after his final attempt to regain control of her – but that didn't stop Eddie from wanting a piece of his father's legacy.

Nathan Conlon had been a complicated man – good looking, charming. He could make you feel like you were the only person in the room. He was also an arrogant, ruthless, selfish narcissist incapable of love. Despite insisting that he loved Grace, he had never shown it in his actions. Perhaps it had been his own abusive childhood that had made him that way, but whatever it was, he was rotten to the core. Grace had always seen some of his traits in her son Jake, but she had also strongly believed that if she gave Jake enough love and affection, enough of her, then his father's less appealing genes would be cancelled out somehow. Seeing him now as the man he had become, she knew that was true. Eddie, however, seemed to have inherited and embodied all of the negative aspects of his father's character, while not retaining any of the positive ones. Upon learning of his true parentage, Eddie set in motion a chain of events that led to him kidnapping Grace with the intention of having her killed, and allowing one of his co-conspirators to rape her in the process. Unsurprisingly, Michael, who hadn't even been her husband back then, had not taken this lightly. He'd found Grace and subsequently tortured Eddie to death.

Grace had cut off all contact with Sandra, who had no doubt gone on wondering what had happened to her son, and hoping that one day he would come home. Grace supposed it was cruel to allow her to suffer like that, but she had no alternative. Protecting her family came above all else. There was no line she wouldn't cross to keep Michael and their children safe.

Grace looked around the kitchen as it became a flurry of activity around her. Suddenly, they had something tangible to get their teeth into rather than the random hit-and-hope approach which had seemed to drive all their attempts at finding Isla up until now. It gave everyone a renewed sense of hope and purpose and she was glad of that. She also believed that Sandra wouldn't physically harm the child. Although her ex-husband Richie had hinted that she wasn't all there right now, Grace still hoped that something of the Sandra she once knew was still there. One thing she did know was that nothing would feel right again until her granddaughter was back home with her family. Nothing would assuage the crushing sense of guilt that was currently threatening to overwhelm her – like an elephant sitting on her chest and refusing to move.

Nathan fucking Conlon!

When would she ever be free of his shadow? He seemed to haunt her as much in death as he had in life, the spectre of him always looming over her life. She straightened her shoulders and cleared her head of any thoughts of him and her past. It was time to exorcise his ghost once and for all.

Chapter Twenty-Six

S uddenly, the whole kitchen was alive with activity. Jazz was on the phone to the florists trying to find out who had placed the order. Connor and John were on their phones alerting all of the search parties that they were now looking for Sandra Redman, while Luke and Danny were trawling the internet to see if they could find any recent information on her. Grace sat at the table with Michael, Jake and Siobhan.

'The last I knew, she lived in Waterloo with that guy she married, Richie,' Grace said, trying to jog her own memory. She had given little thought to her former friend over the last few years. The fact that her son had kidnapped her and almost had her raped and killed had soured that particular friendship. Sandra had reached out to her when Eddie had gone missing, pleading with Grace for help finding him, but she'd brushed her off and they hadn't spoken since. How was Grace supposed to help her look for her missing son, when Eddie had been carved into pieces by her husband? She doubted that even Michael could identify Eddie's final resting place – she'd never asked but he'd alluded to him being scattered across the North-West.

'You remember where, though?' Jake asked.

'No,' Grace shook her head. 'I never went there. Off St John's Road, I think.'

'Dan,' Jake shouted across the kitchen.

'Yeah?'

'Search for Richie Redman too.'

'No, Redman was her maiden name. She still used it for work. Her married name was…' Grace rubbed her temples. It was on the tip of her tongue. 'Harris. He was a mechanic. I'm sure he had his own business.'

'Richie Harris then,' Danny said with a nod, and went back to his laptop.

Grace reached for her son and former daughter-in-law, took each of their hands in hers and squeezed tightly. 'We'll have her home soon. I promise you.'

Jake wrapped his arm around Siobhan's shoulder and she leaned against him as he pressed a soft kiss on her forehead. Michael pushed his chair back and, standing behind Grace, wrapped his arms around her and bent his head low so he could whisper in her ear. 'Those coppers are still outside, so we need to figure out a way for some of us to leave without them following.'

'I know,' she whispered.

It was at that exact moment that Danny looked up from his computer screen and witnessed the scene before him.

Grace and Michael comforting the grieving parents while they clung to each other. Jake and Siobhan – united in their heartache. Each of them knew better than anyone the pain that the other was going through.

It made Danny's heart ache too.

Jazz ended her call and made her way back towards her family gathered around the kitchen table. On seeing that she was off the phone, Connor ended his call too and joined everyone.

'Did you get anything, Jazz?' Jake asked.

'Not much. I might have told the florist that I was a police officer,' she said with a wink, 'and after that she was willing to tell me anything. But she didn't have a lot of information to give. She said the order was placed last night via their website. A gift card was used rather than a credit card so she had no address or anything. And the name on the order was Eddie. That was it. Nothing else.'

'Fuck!' Jake muttered.

'It's okay, we have other leads,' Grace said reassuringly.

'John is directing everyone to make enquiries about Sandra Redman and he'll let us know if anyone comes up with anything,' Connor added.

'You two got anything yet?' Michael asked.

'Hang on one sec,' Luke shouted. He was looking over Danny's shoulder as he typed something into the laptop, and they were both muttering as they peered at the screen.

'Got him!' Danny said and the collective intake of breath rippled around the room.

'Richie Harris has his own garage in Seaforth. Harris's Motors.'

'Original,' Connor murmured.

'Is it open on Sundays?' Grace asked.

'Says seven days a week here,' Danny replied.

'Then we need to get there now and he can take us to his missus,' Connor snarled.

'I can still work on getting her address. I know someone at the council who might be able to help too,' Danny said.

'You think she'll still speak to you after you ghosted her?' Luke asked.

'Just because I'm into fellas now, doesn't mean I'm not still a hit with the ladies,' Danny said with a frown.

'Do what you need to, Dan,' Jake said absent-mindedly as he started pulling on his coat, and Danny felt a twinge of sadness. Ordinarily, Jake was jealous and possessive, and he didn't realise how much comfort he took in that. He silently admonished himself. Isla was missing – of course Jake's entire focus was on finding his daughter.

'Woah,' Michael said to his stepson, putting a firm hand on his shoulder. 'Where do you think you're going?'

'To see Richie Harris,' he snarled.

'No.' Michael shook his head.

'What the fuck?' Jake snarled.

'The police are still outside. There's one car that we can see, but do you think they are not crawling all over this street, waiting for us to make a move? You leave this house and they will be on you like flies on shit.'

'But I can't just sit here when she's out there. Mum?' He turned to Grace, pleading with her.

'Michael's right. Let us deal with it. We'll take two cars and hope they only follow one. Stay here and look after Siobhan. Sean is here if you need anything,' she said, thinking of her brother-in-law and his wife, who had been godsends looking after Belle and Oscar. Sean would love nothing more than to be in the thick of things too, but he was still not fully recovered from being shot a few months earlier. They'd had problems with a rival firm, the Johnson brothers, for a few months. They'd seriously considered themselves contenders to take over the Carter empire, but Grace had been on to them from the start and had even had John Brennan working with them on the inside.

Of the five brothers, only two were still alive – and both of them owed Jake and Connor their lives, which was ironic given that Jake and Connor had murdered their younger brother, Billy. Grace and Michael had managed to pin that murder on the oldest brother, Bradley, who had been double-crossing his brothers all along, while also framing Craig and Ged Johnson for kidnap and attempted murder. It had only been the youngest brother, Scott, who remained at large, and he had tried to avenge his brothers by shooting Michael. The daft sod had shot Sean instead. They'd almost lost him, but he was a tough bastard and even a gunshot to the chest hadn't been enough to see him off. Michael and the boys dealt with Scott in their own unique way and, in order to save their own lives and prove their loyalty, Craig and Ged had killed Bradley. He had dragged them into the whole mess in the first place and then left them to take the fall to save his own skin. He had it coming and his older brothers were aware they were well rid of him.

To his credit, Sean had accepted that his role right now was protecting the other children in the family and Grace was thankful for that, because he usually liked to be in the thick of the action more than anyone.

'Your mum is right, Jake,' Siobhan said as she wrapped her arms around him. 'Stay here.'

Jake shook his head in frustration and then looked over at Danny – the one person who would back him up.

Danny closed his eyes as he spoke. 'You should stay here.'

'Fuck!' Jake shouted and then he sat back down.

'Jazz, can you stay too and keep in contact with John as well as the police? You can get us any updates as they come in.'

'Of course,' Jazz replied.

'Luke, with me and Danny in one car. You and Connor in the other?' Grace suggested to her husband.

He frowned at her. He would much rather be with her and she knew that, but the police were likely to follow one of the cars and either she or Michael needed to be there when they confronted Richie. 'Okay,' he agreed, acquiescing to his wife's common sense.

'Who you think they're gonna follow?' Luke asked.

'Hopefully none of us,' Grace replied.

'Connor and Michael, definitely,' Danny said with a dark laugh.

'You think?' Luke asked.

'They always underestimate a woman,' Grace said, smiling at Danny, who nodded his agreement.

'As soon as we lose them, we'll join you anyway,' Michael said, giving Grace a kiss on the cheek.

'I have no doubt about that.' Then she gave Jake a hug. 'I'll bring her home, son. I promise.'

'I know, Mum,' he whispered and her heart broke for her little boy and the pain he was in.

Chapter Twenty-Seven

A s Grace had known they would, the police officers sitting in the two cars parked outside their house took a great deal of notice as Michael's Jaguar pulled out of the driveway, followed closely by Grace's Mercedes. The unmarked car pulled away from the kerb, following the Jaguar as it turned right and headed down the tree-lined avenue. As Grace turned left, Luke and Danny kept a watch on the patrol car.

'They're on the radio now,' Danny said.

'Probably asking their boss whether they should follow us or stay at the house,' Luke added.

'Let's hope it's the latter,' Grace said as she slipped the car into third gear and drove in the opposite direction.

Checking in her rear-view mirror, she noticed the patrol car hadn't moved. There were no other cars behind her either. She'd hoped that Grosvenor wouldn't have more than two cars outside the house. She was pissed off that he had them there when they should be looking for her granddaughter, but she suspected that he knew they would come up with a viable lead before he did. 'Looks like they're staying put for now,' she said with a smile.

'Yeah. I'll keep my eye out though,' Danny said as he continued looking out of the back window.

As Grace turned onto the main road a call came through on her phone. Pressing the button on her steering wheel to answer, she smiled to herself as DI Grosvenor's voice filled the car.

'A sudden family outing, Mrs Carter?' he asked.

'We need food, Detective Inspector,' she replied. 'I'm just popping to the supermarket. I didn't realise we were under house arrest?'

'Well, no, but when five of you leave at the same time, you can see why that might look suspicious?'

'Not really.'

'And your husband and stepson? Are they headed to the supermarket as well?'

'Well, that would be silly, for us all to go in two different cars, now wouldn't it?'

'Where are they going, Grace?' he asked, the edge creeping into his voice.

'I'm sure the officers in the car you have following them will be able to tell you that, Detective.'

'If you have information pertaining to this case…'

'Like I said, we're just going to pick up some things for dinner. Would your officers like us to bring back anything for them?'

'Any wrong moves now could jeopardise this entire investigation,' he warned.

'This investigation where you're supposed to be finding my granddaughter, but instead you're spending precious time questioning my and my family's movements? That one?'

'I'm warning you, Grace. Don't do anything stupid.'

'Don't threaten me, Detective,' she retorted. 'And I certainly wouldn't be doing anything stupid when my granddaughter is out there somewhere now, would I?' She ended the call and shook her head in annoyance.

'Arsehole,' Danny spat. 'You think I could get away with giving him a good slap when all this is over?'

'He's not worth it, Danny,' Grace reminded him.

'Yeah, but it's still nice to think about though,' he replied.

Grace pressed the button on the steering wheel and called her husband. A few seconds later, Michael's deep voice filled the car instead. 'Anyone following you, love?' he asked.

'It doesn't look like,' Grace replied. 'Grosvenor just called to ask me where we were going.'

'What did you say?'

'Told him we were going shopping. I also told him we knew they were following you. Are they still with you?'

'Yeah. They're still staying a few cars behind, as though they don't stand out like a boil on a fucking arse.'

Grace laughed softly. 'Well, we still can't see anyone, so we're going to head to Richie's garage.'

'Yeah. If I try and lose them then they're going to get suspicious.'

'I know. Why don't you and Connor head to a café or something and wait for us to call you?'

'Yeah, okay,' he said with a sigh. 'Call me as soon as you've spoken to him.'

'I will.'

'Take care of my wife, you two,' Michael said louder, aware he was on speaker phone. 'If anything happens to her…'

Grace rolled her eyes but she couldn't help smiling at the way he was so protective of her. She felt like she was made of titanium with Michael at her side.

'Of course we will, boss,' Danny said with a grin. 'Don't worry, she's safe as houses with me and Luke.'

'She'd better be,' he warned before his tone turned softer again. 'Ring me as soon you can, love. I'll get to you if you need me, okay?'

'Okay. Speak soon. Love you.'

'Love you too.'

She ended the call and focused on the road ahead. 'You have any idea how big this garage is and how many people he might have working for him?' she asked Luke sitting beside her.

'Looks like a fairly small outfit. Maybe one or two people working for him at most, I'd say.'

'Good. Let's hope there aren't too many customers hanging around either,' she replied. 'The quicker we can get this done, the better.'

'Yeah,' Luke agreed.

Richie Harris had his head under the bonnet of an old Ford Mondeo when the brand-new Mercedes pulled up outside his garage. He stood up and brushed his hands over the back of his overalls. Most of his business was word of mouth and it wasn't often he dealt with such fancy motors, but they occasionally rolled in when they'd had a puncture nearby, or the engine light had suddenly come on.

When a smartly dressed woman stepped out of it, followed by two huge, terrifying men, who immediately dropped into step either side of her, he swallowed hard and his sphincter clenched. He had no idea what they were here about, but he could already tell it was nothing to do with a car.

'Richie?' the woman said as she reached him, her eyes scanning the small garage behind him as though she was sizing up the place. It was a Sunday morning and he was in on his own. He'd only started opening on a Sunday a few months ago. It was always quiet, but he had little else to do with his time. He'd thought about staying in bed that morning though, but he'd agreed to take a look at an old mate's alternator. He was beginning to wonder if he was about to regret that decision.

'Yeah,' he replied cautiously.

'Married to Sandra?' she asked.

He rolled his eyes and groaned inwardly. What had that

daft mare done now? He swore she was losing her fucking marbles. 'I was. We're separated,' he replied.

The woman looked toward the little room at the back of the garage that he used as an office and a staff room. 'Can we talk?'

'I thought we already were,' he said and immediately regretted it when a large hand shot out and grabbed him by the throat.

'You have any idea who you're fucking speaking to?' the man with the tattoos all over his arms and the hand on his throat snarled.

Richie tried to shake his head, but the grip on his throat was tight, making it difficult to even breathe. 'No,' he rasped.

The woman put her hand on her attack dog's arm. 'It's okay. Let him go,' she said softly.

The grip on his neck loosened and the man stood back, still glaring at Richie as he did while the second man simply grinned at him – but it was one of the most menacing things he'd ever seen in his life. What the fuck had Sandra dragged him into now?

'Can we talk?' she asked again.

'Yes,' Richie croaked as he rubbed his raw throat. 'Back here.' He turned and walked through the garage to his tiny office. Her heels clicked on the concrete floor as she followed him. He glanced back a few times, making sure none of them had suddenly pulled a gun or a knife and were intending to leave him for dead. He wondered for a second if anyone would miss him and a deep sadness washed over him. He and Sandra had been good together once. He'd tried to be a father to her son, Eddie, but the kid had been feral. He hadn't had an ounce of respect for anyone, least of all his mother. It used to drive Richie mad, the way he spoke to her, but she always defended him – made excuses for why he was the way he was. He had driven a wedge between them and the little fucker had enjoyed every second of it. Then he'd disappeared and Sandra had driven herself crazy trying to find him.

As far as Richie was concerned, it was good riddance to the thieving little shit. The fact that he could muster up no sympathy for the lad's sudden disappearance and possible demise had been the last straw for Sandra. They had limped along together for the next few years, but they'd finally sold the house they'd bought together six months ago and he'd only had the odd call from her since. He knew that back in the day she'd had some powerful friends. He only hoped she hadn't now made them her enemies.

Grace followed Richie into the small room in his garage. The smell of grease and oil reminded her of Nudge's scrapyard and she felt a sudden pang of grief at the loss of her old friend. But the smell was the only similarity. It was clear as she walked through the garage and into the tiny office that Richie took good care of the place. Tools were secured in huge red tool chests. Tyres were neatly racked on shelves and his small room had three padded chairs, a computer and a small, clean kitchenette.

Richie indicated the cleanest of the three chairs as two of them had oil stains on from where he and his colleague obviously sat. 'That's for guests,' he said as though reading her mind. 'If you'd like to sit.'

'Thank you,' she said with a smile. She was desperate for information, but she was experienced enough to know that you can catch far more flies with honey. The room was only big enough for three of them really, so Luke waited outside the door, keeping a watchful eye in case anyone cared to walk in.

'Is there something I can help you with?' he asked her.

'Where's Sandra?'

He blinked at her and his mouth opened but he didn't speak.

'She asked you a question,' Danny snarled.

'I-I don't know,' Richie replied as the colour began to drain from his face.

'You know where she lives?' Grace asked.

He narrowed his eyes at her. 'Why do you need to know? Is she in trouble?'

'Yes,' Grace replied honestly.

'What kind of trouble?' he asked as his hands started to tremble.

'Her address, Richie?' she asked again, her patience already wearing thin.

'T-tell me why you want to know,' he stammered.

Grace sighed deeply before she looked up at Danny. That was all the permission he needed. He took one step towards Richie and grabbed him by the throat again, this time pulling him from his seat. He squeezed tightly until the other man's face began turning purple. He clawed at

Danny's forearm as he struggled but he was no match for the younger man's strength.

'Enough now,' Grace said quietly and Danny released him, throwing him back into his chair. Then he planted a hand on each armrest before leaning his face close to Richie's. 'My boss is going to ask you some questions. You're going to answer every single one without hesitation. And if you don't, or I think you're not telling the truth, I'm going to start cutting off parts of you. Do you understand me?'

Richie stared up at him, his eyes full of terror as a wet stain spread through the crotch of his overalls. 'Okay,' he nodded and Danny stepped back into his position standing behind Grace.

'When was the last time you saw Sandra?' she asked.

'I can't remember.' Richie shook his head. Danny sucked in a breath that made Richie jump. 'I mean I really can't. It's been months.'

'When was the last time you spoke to her then?'

'About three weeks ago. She didn't sound good, to be honest.'

'In what way?'

'She was rambling on about her son, Eddie, about our wedding, how we should have had some kids of our own. I thought she might be drunk, but she swore she wasn't. I think she's having some kind of breakdown, to be honest. She was never the same after Eddie disappeared.'

'Has she ever mentioned any plans to you about revenge for his disappearance?'

'No. She was obsessed with finding him for a few years and then I think…' he trailed off.

'You think?' she prompted him.

'I think she started to believe he was dead. I mean, he hadn't come crawling back for money, so…' he said with a shrug. 'Like I said, it wasn't the same after he went missing. I begged her to see the doctor and get some help, but she point-blank refused.'

'Where does she live now?'

'She's got a flat in Old Swan. I have the address on my phone somewhere.'

'We're going to be needing that,' Grace said.

Richie nodded, taking his phone from the table beside him and opening it up.

'Can I ask what kind of trouble she's in?' he asked quietly. 'I mean, we're not together, but she's… she's not been the same since Eddie disappeared.'

'Has she ever spoken to you before about her desire to have more children?' she asked.

'Not for years. She couldn't have any more. We tried after we were married for a while, but…' His voice cracked with emotion.

Grace nodded her understanding. She hadn't been aware of that. 'What about other people's children? She ever tried to take someone else's, or talked about it?'

'What?' Richie frowned at her. 'No. She would never…'

'Well, it seems like she has, Richie,' she replied.

She watched his Adam's apple bob in his throat as he swallowed. 'Is that what she's done? Taken your child?' He whispered the words as though he was horrified by them and it was then that Grace realised he genuinely had no idea what was going on here. If Sandra had taken Isla, then Richie had no part in it.

'My granddaughter,' Grace replied.

'I'm sorry,' Richie said with genuine sorrow.

Grace sat back in the chair. If Sandra had taken Isla from the soft play centre, then she must have taken a child with her in the first place. You didn't get to just walk into those places on your own without looking all kinds of strange and being asked to leave. 'Does Sandra have any nieces or nephews? Any children she looks after for a friend, maybe?'

Richie shook his head. 'None that I'm aware of.' Then he looked back at his phone screen. 'I have her address here if you want to write it down.'

'Give me the phone,' Danny demanded and Richie handed it over. Danny took a photo of it before handing it back.

'We got her number too,' he said to Grace who gave him a faint smile in acknowledgment.

'Does Sandra have anywhere else that she likes to stay, or visit? A caravan maybe or a friend's place?'

'No. Not that I know of, anyway.'

'Thank you for your time,' Grace said as she stood up. Then she placed a hand on Danny's shoulder. She didn't have to speak for him to know what he was supposed to do next – he knew the score.

Grace left the room and walked to the car, leaving Danny and Luke alone with Richie. He needed to know that their conversation had to be a secret he would take to his grave.

———

Richie shrank back in his chair, cowering and trembling in fear, as Danny Alexander advanced on him. Luke remained in the doorway, keeping half an eye on Grace in the car and half on Danny. He wasn't needed to help deliver this particular message. In fact, even having Danny do it was akin to using a sledgehammer to crack a peanut.

'W-what? I t-told you where sh-she is,' Richie stammered.

'I know that,' Danny said with a menacing smile. 'But we need to make sure that you know exactly who we are and what we do to people who don't keep our secrets, Richie.'

'I know. I won't say anything. I swear,' Richie whimpered, closing his eyes as though it might prevent whatever terrible thing was about to happen.

Danny pulled the small flick knife from his coat pocket with one hand as he took hold of Richie's jaw with the other. 'I know you won't,' he snarled as he held the tip of the blade directly below Richie's eye, pressing it lightly until the tip pierced the skin and drew blood.

'Argh!' Richie screamed and tried to squirm but Danny held him firmly in his grip.

'Careful,' he said with a sneer. 'If you struggle too much, you might lose an eye.'

At those words, Richie stilled, his face pale and his eyes wide as he stared up into the face of his attacker.

Danny drew the blade a few centimetres along Richie's cheekbone. 'Now every time you look in the mirror, you will remember me and what I do to people who cross me or my bosses, Richie. Because if you tell anyone what happened here today, this little cut on your face,' Danny pressed the tip of the blade a little deeper and Richie cried out, 'will be the least of your worries. Do you understand me?'

'Y-yes,' Richie snivelled as he stared into Danny's dark eyes. 'I won't say a word.'

'Good boy.' Danny winked at him before wiping the blade on Richie's overalls and putting it back into his pocket. 'You should really get that cut looked at, though. It will probably need a few stitches. How the fuck did you manage to do that to yourself?'

Richie blinked at him for a few seconds before the penny dropped. 'I was cutting some cable and the knife slipped,' he whispered.

Danny nodded in satisfaction before turning on his heel and walking out of the small room with Luke.

'You think he'll keep his mouth shut?' Danny asked as they reached the car.

'I think he just shat his pants, Dan. He's not going to want to come to our attention again any time soon.'

'Yeah,' Danny replied, happy that he'd dealt with the situation with minimal bloodshed and maximum effect, just like Grace Carter expected.

When he and Luke climbed into the car a moment later, she simply smiled at them both. She didn't ask any questions about what had happened after she'd left, trusting that they had taken care of it. Something about that, and the faith she had in him, made Danny's chest swell with pride.

Chapter Twenty-Eight

S andra Redman folded the pink cardigan and placed it
on top of the suitcase. It was probably a little too big
for Isla, but it would have to do. Her neighbours from two
doors down, Fiona and Jack, had two daughters, and had
been kind enough to donate some of the clothes they'd
grown out of to the charity shop where Sandra worked. She
hadn't taken them in though, keeping them in her wardrobe
instead – just in case. She reasoned that Fiona and Jack had
obviously meant for her to keep them, but they just didn't
want her to feel uncomfortable. They must have known it
was only a matter of time before a child came into her life.
She smiled to herself, warmed by their generosity, which
meant that Isla had a small wardrobe of two cardigans, four
dresses, two pairs of dungarees, a pair of jeans, a few T-
shirts and two pairs of pyjamas. It had been harder to get
her some socks and underwear, but she would order some
online as soon as they got to Devon.

It had all been thanks to Fiona and Jack that she had Isla at all. Their oldest daughter, Freya, was sixteen and used to look after her seven-year old sister, Rosie, every Saturday morning while their parents worked. But when Freya got herself a Saturday job, Fiona was talking about having to cut back her hours, or even change jobs. That was when Sandra offered to help out. She hadn't been living next door long, but she'd been to dinner with her neighbours plenty of times and she knew both girls well. At first, she would watch Rosie at her own house playing tea parties with her dolls. But when the new soft play opened on the retail estate where Fiona worked, she suggested taking Rosie there. She paid of course and Sandra got to relax with a cup of coffee while secretly pretending that Rosie was her daughter. It was just a fantasy though – she wasn't harming anyone.

That was how she and Rosie came to be regulars at Charlie's soft play every Saturday morning. When Rosie had brought a new friend to Sandra's table, and that friend had dark hair and the same blue eyes as her father and grandfather, and had confidently announced her name was Isla Conlon, Sandra had felt like somebody had handed her a winning lottery ticket. Isla had been delighted when Sandra had told her that she knew her nanna and grandad, and her daddy. She had told the little girl all about how they were just like family really, given that her Uncle Eddie was Daddy's brother.

So when Sandra suggested Rosie invite Isla back to Rosie's house for a tea party, like any excited seven-year-old would, she'd said yes. Isla wanted to tell her great-grandpa

Pat and great-grandma Sue though – that had been a problem. But Sandra had managed to convince the child that she had their phone number and would call them to collect her when she was done. Rosie had been so excited to make a friend and have her over for a tea party that she'd played her part spectacularly. Sandra already knew that the CCTV didn't cover the entrance because of an incident a few weeks earlier involving two cars having a minor bump in the car park.

Provided she could get the girl out with minimum fuss, she would be home and dry. She'd signed in with a fake name. She always did. She liked to invent a new persona every week and this week she'd been Imelda Macrón – a dancer from Paris. She giggled to herself at the thought. By the time the police wanted to interview Imelda and then realised she didn't exist, Sandra and Isla would be in Torquay. She'd been there once with Richie. It was a beautiful place. A great place to bring up a child. Isla would be better off with her, of that she had no doubt.

Jake Conlon was a gangster. A villain and a womaniser – just like his father had been. What kind of life was he giving his daughter? Sandra knew one thing. She could offer her a better one. She could be a mother to the girl. It was only fair after she had been denied the right to be a mother again herself. The Carters had taken Eddie from her, she knew it. Terrified that her son would stake a claim on the Carter empire, Jake had got rid of the threat and that bitch of a mother of his had covered up for him. They deserved to know the pain and suffering of losing a child. They deserved to go to sleep every single night and stare at the walls while imagining their baby out there suffering and in pain.

That was why she'd sent the flowers. She just had to let them know she was the cause of their suffering. She had to do it for Eddie. What would be the point otherwise? She'd been careful though. She couldn't be too obvious because she knew the police would be snooping around. She only hoped they understood her cryptic message.

'Sandy, when is my nanny coming for me?' Isla whined as she walked into the bedroom.

Sandra closed the suitcase and took a deep breath. She hoped the whining would stop soon. Eddie never whined like that. After they'd been at Rosie's for a while, she'd taken Isla to her flat and told her to wait until Fiona had come home. She knew that Isla's disappearance would be on the news and she didn't want her asking any unnecessary questions. When she'd got back to the flat, she'd told Isla that there had been an emergency and she was going to look after her for the night while her mum and dad were busy. The girl had cried about that and even ice-cream hadn't placated her. Eventually, after Sandra had talked to her about how she had looked after her father when he was a little boy, the child had finally settled and had fallen asleep with tear-stained cheeks – after a spoonful of Night Nurse, something that always made Sandra sleep too.

Earlier that morning, when Isla had finally woken up, Sandra had told her about the trip they needed to take so that she could hand her over to her grandparents. She hoped that in time, the girl would simply stop asking questions and accept that her new life was better than her old one. She would see that as soon as they got to Torquay and she saw the beach.

'Soon. I told you. We're going on a little trip and your nanny Grace is going to meet us when we get there.'

'And Grandad?'

'Yes, and your grandad.'

'But what about my mummy and daddy?' the girl pouted as she threw herself on the bed. 'I want to see them.'

'And you will, angel, just as soon as we get there. They're all waiting for you,' she snapped, the edge creeping into her voice. Perhaps she should give her another dose of Night Nurse? Make the girl sleep during the car ride to Torquay?

Chapter Twenty-Nine

Fiona Walker looked out of her window to see her neighbour loading up her car.

'Looks like Sandra is going on a trip,' she said as she sipped her coffee.

'Hmm,' her husband Jack replied absent-mindedly as he read the morning paper.

'Did Sandra mention she was going anywhere, Rosie?' she asked her daughter as she walked to the table and ruffled her hair. Selfishly, she hoped that Sandra would be back before the weekend. They had come to rely on her so much on Saturdays when they both had to work.

Jack closed the paper and the cute face of the little girl who'd gone missing yesterday from the soft play where Sandra took Rosie stared back at her. It made Fiona's heart constrict in her chest at what the girl and her parents must be going through, and she bent to give Rosie a kiss on the head, thankful that her own children were safe and well.

'I hope she's found soon,' she whispered to Jack, who nodded his agreement.

'So close to home,' he agreed. 'I don't want Rosie going there anymore, babe.'

'I agree,' she said with a shudder. She had left work and been doing the weekly shop at the supermarket when everything had happened, so the first she knew of the missing girl was on the Saturday teatime news. Fortunately, Rosie had been out of the room. She preferred to shield her children from the horrors of the world, and according to Sandra, it had all happened after they'd left.

'You've met her grandparents, right?' she said. Jack worked at Sophia's Kitchen restaurant, which just happened to be owned by Grace and Michael Carter, the missing girl's grandparents.

'Yeah. Nice people,' he said with a nod.

Fiona smiled. Everyone knew who the Carters were, but lots of people worked for them in their legitimate business and found them to be fair employers who paid well.

Rosie looked up from her Coco Pops and pulled the newspaper towards her. 'That's Isla,' she squealed. 'She's my new best friend.'

Fiona looked at her husband in horror.

'Missing?' Rosie blinked at the two of them. She was able to read and the headline was easy to read even upside down. 'What does that mean, Mummy?'

Fiona crouched down as her heart started to hammer in her chest. She'd been distracted yesterday when Rosie had been talking about her and Sandra playing tea parties with her new best friend. Rosie and Sandra often made up imaginary names and friends and Fiona had assumed that was what she'd been talking about.

'Where did you meet Isla, darling?' she asked softly, careful to keep her voice steady.

'At Charlie's. I told you.' She shook her head in righteous indignation.

'Yes, you did. And after Charlie's? Did you see her again?'

'Yes!' She folded her little arms across her chest. 'She came here to play tea parties. I told you.'

Fiona glanced at Jack, whose face was now the colour of his light-grey T-shirt.

'And then where did she go, sweetheart?'

'Sandra took her home.'

'She took her home?'

'Yes,' Rosie said and frowned.

'Did you go too?'

'No. She only went to her house.'

'Sandra took Isla to her house?'

'Yes. I watched her out of the window,' Rosie replied.

Fiona's hand flew to her mouth, as she thought she might throw up. 'Jack, we need to call the police.'

'Fuck that, Fiona. We need to call my boss. We've all had instructions to call in if we see anything at all.'

'But that little girl,' she whispered, covering Rosie's ears.

'You think they won't deal with this quicker than the police can?' he asked. 'If they find out she was in our house and we didn't tell them…' He shook his head. 'They're only good people if you don't cross them, Fiona.'

She considered everything for a second. Her family were the most important thing in the world to her. Sandra was in deep trouble, but then that was her own fault for going off and kidnapping the daughter of one of the most dangerous men in Liverpool – what did she expect?

'Call them,' she agreed.

Fiona ushered Rosie into the living room to watch TV while Jack called Lena, his boss at Sophia's Kitchen. She heard the tail end of his side of the conversation as she walked back into the room.

'What now?' she asked as he was searching through his phone.

'She said to call Danny directly. She's sent me his number,' he mumbled as he dialled the next number.

'Who's he?'

'He's the security boss. Jake's partner.'

'I thought that was Connor?'

'Not his business partner, babe,' he snapped as he held the phone to his ear.

'Oh, right.' Fiona sat down opposite her husband and took hold of his hand, giving it a reassuring squeeze. Then she listened to his side of the call.

'Danny, it's Jack Walker. I work in Sophia's Kitchen. Lena gave me your number. I think I know where Isla is.'

'At the house of one of our neighbours.'

'Lemmington Road. We're at seventy-four so she'd be at seventy-two.'

'She took our daughter to that soft play place yesterday. It appears that she brought Isla back with them too. My kid's seven. We've only just pieced it together, now she's seen Isla's photo in the paper.'

'You are? Good. It looks like she's getting ready to leave.'

'Okay. Will do.'

He'd ended the call and put his phone on the table. 'He said that they're already on their way, but he asked me to make sure she doesn't leave.'

Fiona stood up and walked to the window. 'And how do we do that?'

'By force if I have to, Fiona,' he said as he joined her, his hand resting on the small of her back. 'She kidnapped someone's fucking kid.'

'I know,' she whispered.

'And we let her into our house. Let her look after Rosie.' He shook his head in disbelief.

'She seemed so nice, though. I mean, a little quirky, but nice.'

'You don't think she's hurt her, do you?' he asked.

'No. She wouldn't do that,' she said with conviction, hoping that she was right.

Chapter Thirty

D anny slipped the phone back into his pocket.

'Who was that?' Grace asked him as she turned in her seat. Luke was driving now, while Grace co-ordinated a pick-up of Michael from the café he and Connor were waiting at, as well as a distraction for the police who were still waiting outside, watching him and Connor.

'Some fella who works for us, also happens to be a neighbour of Sandra's. Said she took his daughter to that soft play yesterday and brought Isla home too.'

'So she *is* with Sandra then?' Grace heaved a sigh of relief. 'That's good to know.' She had to admit she'd been worried, going solely by the card with the flowers. It could have all been a red herring.

'Yeah. Michael gonna meet us there?' he asked.

'Yes. John is picking him up. Then I'll only need one of you to stay. Can one of you go back with John and take Isla with you?'

'I'll take her,' Danny said, anxious to get the little girl he'd come to love so much back to her parents.

'Good.'

'How are we going to handle this, Grace? I mean, this is a residential street. There will be witnesses,' Luke said.

'We get Isla out first and then Michael and I will deal with Sandra while you stay outside and watch for any signs of trouble – or the police.'

'Okay,' Luke agreed.

A few minutes later, Luke pulled the car to a stop outside 74 Lemmington Road, the home of Jack Walker. Grace climbed out of the car as Jack came to the kerb to greet them. She recognised him immediately. He was a good waiter and a hard worker.

'If we had realised sooner, Grace...' he said apologetically.

'I know,' she said. 'Thank you for calling us and not the police.'

He nodded his understanding.

'Is she still in there?' she asked.

'Yeah. Me and Fiona, that's my wife, we've been watching. She's been filling her car up and she went back into the house a couple of minutes ago.'

'Anyone else in those flats?'

'Not right now. Top one is empty and Nick and Mal are on holiday. Sandra's is the ground floor.'

'Okay. Are you going to be around for the next hour? My brother will speak to you about what happens next. You know Luke, right?' she asked as he stepped out of the car along with Danny.

Jack visibly blanched and Grace placed a reassuring hand on his arm. 'You have absolutely nothing to worry about, Jack. My family are in your debt.'

'I'll be around, yeah,' he said.

'Good,' she said and then she turned sharply as John Brennan's distinctive BMW X5 pulled up behind her car.

'I thought you two were being discreet?' she said as he and Michael jumped out.

'I'm not sure John knows the meaning of the word, love,' Michael said with an arch of one eyebrow as he reached her, sliding an arm around her waist. 'Shall we do this?'

'Let's,' she replied and they walked the few metres to Sandra's flat.

The door to the main house was open and Grace, Michael and Danny walked straight in while Luke and John waited outside.

When they reached the door to Sandra's flat, Danny smiled. 'This will be no problem,' he said as he took out his small multi-tool and picked the lock.

The door was an old one with an old fashioned Yale lock which gave way easily.

'Shall we?' Danny asked with a wink as he pushed the door open and allowed Michael and Grace to step inside. He followed close behind as they made their way down the small hallway and into the living room.

Isla was sitting on the sofa clutching a doll to her chest. 'Nanny! Grandad!' she shouted as she saw them walk into the room.

'Hello, princess.' Michael beamed when he saw her, dropping to his knees and holding his arms wide. She ran into them and he scooped her up, smothering her face with kisses as she clung to him. Then she looked up at Grace and launched herself into her arms.

'Sweetheart,' Grace said, holding back the tears and burying her face in Isla's hair. The relief at holding her and seeing her safe was indescribable.

'Sandy told me we were going to see you,' Isla sniffed. 'I thought she was lying. She said she was your friend.'

At that point, Sandra walked into the room from the back of the flat. She stared at the people before her, her mouth twisted in anger.

'That's right, sweetheart. Sandy here is a very old friend of mine. Did she look after you for me?'

'She did,' Isla admitted. 'She let me have ice-cream for breakfast,' she giggled.

Grace let out an exaggerated gasp of horror. 'She did?'

'Yeah.' Isla grinned at her.

'Hey, munchkin,' Danny said from behind them and Isla almost knocked Grace over trying to get to him.

'Danny,' she squeaked in delight as he gave her a huge hug.

'Danny's going to take you home to our house, sweetheart,' Grace said as she stroked her granddaughter's hair. 'Your mum and dad are waiting there for you.'

'Are you and Grandad coming too?' Isla pouted. 'You're not going back to Spain, are you?'

'No.' Grace smiled at her. 'We'll be home shortly.'

'Okay. Bye, Sandy,' Isla called as she took hold of Danny's hand and allowed him to lead her out of the room and to the safety of John's car.

As Danny closed the front door behind him Sandra Redman sank to her knees. Even in her deluded frame of mind, she knew it was the end of the line for her.

'You planning a trip somewhere, *Sandy*?' Grace asked.

'Fuck off, bitch!' Sandra spat.

Michael dropped the rucksack he was holding to the floor and began taking out the things he needed. Once he knew that John was picking him up, he'd given him specific instructions about what he'd need to put an end to this whole mess once and for all.

'Why did you do it? She's just a baby. She's innocent,' Grace said.

'My baby was innocent too,' Sandra sniffed. 'My Eddie.'

'Eddie? Innocent?' Grace scoffed. 'He was a piece of shit, Sandra, and you know it.'

Sandra pushed herself to her feet. 'He could have been somebody. He could have had that club if only Nathan had been allowed to be a father to him, but you wouldn't have it, would you? Selfish bitch!'

Grace sighed. Sandra had lost the plot and the one thing she had learned in all her years was that you couldn't argue with stupid – or crazy. It was just a waste of energy. If Sandra wanted to rewrite history in her own head than that was up to her. She didn't remind her that Nathan had threatened to kill both her and her baby if she ever told anyone the kid was his. Or how he'd paid her off to keep quiet. How he'd begged Grace for forgiveness time and time again – because Sandra wasn't the only woman he'd used and discarded. She wasn't the only one he'd got pregnant either – who knew how many abortions that man had been responsible for?

'You deserve to suffer for what you've put my family through over the last twenty-four hours, Sandra,' she said instead. 'But fortunately for you, the police are going to be crawling all over this place soon enough, so I'm offering you an out.'

Sandra wasn't so deluded that she didn't realise what that was. 'What?' she asked with a scowl.

It was then that Michael held up the rubber ligature and the syringe in his gloved hands. 'You put this in your own arm and slip away peacefully.'

'Fuck you!' she snapped. 'Why would I make this easy for you?'

Grace walked over to her and, grabbing the woman by her hair, yanked her head back and looked in her eyes. 'Because if you don't, my husband and I will drive you to our lock-up on the docks. Then he will spend the next few days making you suffer, Sandra, while I watch. Michael knows every way there is to cause pain. It was kind of his thing back in the day. First he'll start with your fingernails – pulling them out one by one. Then he'll do the same to your toenails. Once he's done, he'll start on your teeth. Pulling each one out one at a time. Can you imagine how much that will hurt? Having them ripped out by a pair of rusty pliers?' Grace shuddered at the thought.

Sandra's face was grey but she didn't give in.

'Then the real pain will begin. He'll start slicing things off. Your toes. Your ears. Your eyelids. Your nipples. Your tongue,' Grace hissed.

'Stop it!' Sandra shrieked as she covered her ears.

'Then when you think you can't take any more pain, he'll give you some morphine to take the edge off and some adrenaline to make you feel like you've got a chance to get away,' Grace pulled her head back harder. 'Before he crushes every single bone in your body.'

She let go of Sandra's hair, letting her fall to the floor. 'I'm happy either way, Sandra. The likelihood is we'll be able to pay people off to cover up what we do to you, but you took one of mine –' she spat '– and I will happily do a life sentence to make you pay.'

Sandra stared up at her. 'Did he suffer? Did my Eddie suffer like that?'

Michael handed Grace the syringe and the ligature. 'You'll never know unless you ask him yourself,' she said, holding them out to Sandra.

After a few seconds, Sandra took them with trembling hands. 'I don't know how to…' she snivelled.

'That's okay, Michael will help you.'

'Come on, eh?' Michael said softly as he took her by her elbow and led her to the sofa. 'Think of it like going for a nice sleep. This shit will feel amazing when it kicks in.'

She looked at him. His face was full of compassion and concern and it seemed to calm her somehow. She sat on the sofa, putting her feet up on the cushions.

'It won't hurt?' she whispered, her words and body trembling.

'Not even a little bit,' Michael assured her. 'Give me your arm.'

She held it out for him and he took it gently in his hands before wrapping the ligature around the top of her arm. He handed her one end of the rubber tube. 'Pull this tight,' he ordered and she complied, seemingly transfixed by him.

Grace watched him work. He was careful that the ligature wasn't so tight that she couldn't have fixed it herself. The way he helped her could almost be described as tender. Sandra stared into his dark-brown eyes as though he was her saviour and not her killer.

He tapped her arm gently and found a vein. 'Here.' He showed her how to hold the syringe. 'Just press it here.' He rubbed a gloved finger over the vein. 'It will scratch but then you press the plunger and it will be the best feeling of your life.'

'You promise?' she breathed.

'I promise,' he said with a nod and a reassuring smile.

Sandra's hand trembled as she pressed the needle against her arm but with Michael's gentle words of encouragement she pierced the skin, pressed the plunger and injected herself with enough morphine to take out a horse.

It was only when all of the drugs were in her system,

and she had her head lolled back and a goofy smile on her face, that he spoke again.

'Sandra, you still with us?'

'Yeah,' she mumbled.

'Good.' Michael's tone had changed and the soft, soothing voice was replaced by a cold, menacing one. 'I want you to know that your son was a vile piece of shit and he spent his last hours screaming in agony while I broke and burned every single part of his body.'

Sandra's smile faltered and her eyes rolled in her head.

Michael turned to his wife. 'You okay?'

'I am now.'

He walked over to her and wrapped his arms around her as she melted against his broad chest. 'Thank you,' she whispered.

'Anything for you, love. You know that,' he breathed against her hair.

She smiled. She did know that. He would die for her and their children. Meanwhile, Sandra Redman slipped away in a trance. Her son had spent his final moments in pain, and the knowledge haunted her own.

Luke Sullivan sat across from Jack and Fiona Walker with a mug of tea before him. That seemed to be the Scouse answer to every situation. Somebody died – have a cup of tea. You get dumped – have a cup of tea. You find out your neighbour kidnapped your boss's daughter – have a cup of tea.

'You're a good worker, Jack. Grace values that, and she also values loyalty. You've shown that today, but we need a little more.'

'W-what do you need me to do?'

'The police are eventually going to figure out it was Sandra who took Isla. They're probably closing in on her now. Ten minutes after I leave here, you're going to call them and tell them that your neighbour has been acting suspiciously and you think she kidnapped the girl from the news. You saw her packing her car and when you spoke to her she started crying and telling you she'd made a huge mistake. You're going to tell them that she said, *I've taken her back, but it's not enough. Tell them I'm sorry.* Then she went into her house. It was then that you came home and spoke to Rosie, who told you whatever it was that made you pick up the phone and call us today. But you never called us and we were never here. Okay?'

'Okay.' Jack nodded. 'And Sandra?'

'She'll be in her flat because you haven't seen her leave, have you?'

'No.' Both Jack and Fiona shook their heads.

'The only lies you tell are the ones I just gave you. Everything else is the truth. Is that clear?' he asked. His tone was sharper, but he needed to know they got the message.

'Crystal. You can count on us,' Jack assured him.

Luke looked at Fiona. 'Yes,' she agreed. 'Of course you can.'

As Michael drove back to their house in Mossley Hill, Grace dialled Andy Dixon's number. Unusually, he answered instead of letting it go to voicemail.

'I'm working on it,' he said.

'I don't need it anymore. We have her. She's safe.'

'Thank Christ for that. Where? Who?'

'It doesn't matter. But I didn't want you to go getting into trouble for something I no longer need.'

'Trouble? Me? Nah!' he laughed.

'Thank you though.'

'Even though I didn't come through in time?'

'All that matters is that she's safe.'

'Yeah,' he agreed.

Grace sucked in a breath. They never spoke about Marcus. It was too painful for both of them, but she had to tell him the truth. 'He would want you to be happy, Andy. He was that kind of person.'

'How do I let myself be happy with anyone, Grace, when I couldn't do it for him? The best man I ever knew?'

'Because nothing in this life matters if you don't have someone to share it with, Andy. He loved you until his dying day, but he still lived. He was still open to love, even if he never quite found what you two had. He only wanted you to be happy. You have to know that.'

'I do,' he whispered.

'Good.'

'Does this mean I still owe you?' he asked, defusing the tension.

'Always.'

He laughed out loud at that. 'Bye, Grace.'

'Bye, Andy.'

'Who was that?' Michael asked when she ended the call.

'A very old friend with very big connections,' she said with a smile.

He raised his eyebrows at her. 'Anyone I need to worry about?'

She placed a hand on his cheek. 'You?' she breathed. 'You never have to worry about anyone.'

'Too fucking right,' he said with a wink, making her laugh.

Chapter Thirty-One

J ake was standing on the steps of his mum's house. He rocked on the balls of his feet, his hands stuffed in his pockets and his heart hammering in his chest. He'd never been so anxious and so full of nervous energy in all his life. Danny had Isla with him and he knew that she was safe, but until he held his little girl in his arms he couldn't relax.

Siobhan stood beside him, clasping his arm tightly as she chewed on her lip and picked at the sleeve of her cardigan with her other hand. Connor stood behind them, his presence solid and comforting.

When John Brennan's car turned into the driveway, Jake ran down the steps and onto the driveway, opening the car door as soon as he heard John switch off the child locks. He pulled open the door. 'Mummy! Daddy!' Isla shrieked.

Pulling her out of the car, he wrapped her in his arms as

Siobhan threw her arms around her too. He smoothed her hair, kissing her head over and over again as she giggled at the attention from her parents. To his relief, she seemed absolutely fine. Who knew the lasting impact this whole situation would have on her, but he would deal with that in the future. Right now she was here and she was safe and happy. He'd never prayed or believed in any kind of God – but despite that he said a silent prayer of thanks.

Siobhan Conlon clung onto her daughter and her ex-husband as though she might never let them go. The last twenty-eight hours had been complete hell. The thought that her baby was out there somewhere, crying for her mum and wondering why she wasn't there, had been like a knife twisting in her heart. For the first time in twenty-eight long hours, she felt like she could actually breathe. She placed her cheek against Isla's hair. She smelled sweet and the thought that the woman who had taken her might have washed her daughter's hair made her stomach twist in a knot.

But then she felt a strong hand on her neck as Jake pulled her closer, until Isla was pressed tightly between them. She stole a glance at him and her heart swelled in her chest. No matter what had happened between them in the past, he had been there for her in a way that no one else ever had and nobody ever would. She wiped away a tear as she thought how much she still loved him. There was no sexual attraction any longer, even though her love for him had once burned white-hot; what they had instead was a deep, lasting friendship.

'Thank you,' she whispered and he winked at her in response.

'I'm hungry, Mummy,' Isla said as she wriggled between them both, making them laugh.

'What do you want to eat, princess? You can have anything you like.'

Isla lifted her head and smiled cheekily at them both. 'Anything?'

'Anything,' Jake agreed.

'Cupcakes with pink frosting,' Isla squealed. 'The ones with unicorns and sprinkles on that Jazz makes.'

'We'd better get inside and ask her then,' Siobhan said with a laugh.

'Shall we go inside, sweetheart? Everyone has missed you,' Jake said.

'Yeah. But I can walk, you know, Dad,' she pouted as he started to carry her inside. Siobhan rolled her eyes. Their daughter was too independent for her own good.

'Okay.' He laughed as he put her down. He wrapped an arm around Siobhan's waist as they watched their daughter run into the house after her grandparents. She stopped when she reached Danny, who had got out of the car and walked to the doorway, and she held out her arms for a hug. He responded by bending and scooping her up, making her squeal with laughter again.

'You think she has any idea what she's been through?' Siobhan whispered.

'It doesn't seem like. Thank fuck!' Jake replied.

'Hmm.' She leaned her head on his shoulder. 'She adores Danny, you know.'

'Yeah,' Jake said with a grin. She wasn't the only one.

Chapter Thirty-Two

Jake found Siobhan standing near the kitchen sink at his mum's house, staring out of the window. Isla had been back for two days and both she and Siobhan, as well as he and Danny, had remained at his mum's house since. It had seemed like the most natural thing to do – to be surrounded by family after such a traumatic event. He was planning on going back to his own place as soon as possible. He loved being at his mum and Michael's house, and being close to Connor and Jazz down the road, but he and Danny needed their own space.

He wondered how long Siobhan planned on staying. He knew his mum and Michael would never ask her to leave, but would she ever do so if they didn't? What had happened to their daughter had understandably shaken Siobhan to her core, but he sensed there was something else going on with her too.

'Hey, you okay?' he asked as he walked toward her.

She turned to him, blinking in surprise as though he'd just snapped her from a deep dream. 'What? I was miles away.'

'I asked if you were okay,' he repeated, reaching out and placing a hand on her shoulder.

A fat tear ran down her face and she brushed it away quickly as though she hoped he wouldn't see.

'Siobhan,' he said softly as he wrapped his arms around her. She pressed her face against his chest and started to sob. Jake held onto her, wondering what else he could do, given that she seemed so fragile lately. He suspected it wasn't entirely down to what had happened to Isla. When she stopped crying, he guided her to a chair and poured her a glass of water.

Sitting opposite her, he watched as she wrapped her hands around the glass.

'Is there something else going on, Siobhan?' he asked.

She looked at him, her eyes red and puffy from crying. 'I'm pregnant, Jake.'

'Oh.' He blinked at her in shock. That was the last thing he'd expected to hear and he didn't know what question to ask first, but she saved him from having to by telling him everything.

'It was some guy I met at the wine bar. He seemed really sweet and charming. We used protection but, you know it's not foolproof.' She wiped another tear from her eye and then stared at him. 'And I actually did use protection, not like when we were together and I pretended to.' Her cheeks flushed pink at her admission.

'Best thing to ever happen to me,' he replied with a wink, thinking only of their beautiful daughter, although when he'd found out about her deception, he'd been furious.

'Anyway, when I found out, I told him and that was when he told me he was married with four kids already.'

'Four? Fuck, Siobhan! And married! How old was he?'

'Thirty-six. Not that much older than me. And it's not like we were serious, but he did tell me he was single. He told me to get rid of it and that he never wanted to see me again,' she sniffed.

Jake shook his head in annoyance. He could just imagine the smarmy, arrogant fucker, cheating on his wife and leaving Siobhan to deal with a kid on her own. 'You want me to fuck him up?'

'God, no.' She shook her head and laughed softly. 'I never want to see him again. He's a prick. I don't want him anywhere near my baby, but...'

'But?'

'I just feel so alone, Jake.' She started to cry again and he pushed back his chair and went around the table to comfort her.

'You're not alone, babe. You've got me and Isla, and Danny, and my mum and everyone else.'

'Thank you.' She smiled at him. 'But it's not the same as having someone at home every night to talk about your day, make you a cup of tea or just get you a glass of water when you're feeling down.' She held up the glass he'd just given her.

'You'll meet someone, Siobhan, when the time is right.'

'That's such a cliché.' She laughed and pushed him playfully in the chest.

'True, though. Look at me and Danny. I thought I'd never find anyone I loved as much as Paul...'

'Yeah. He's such a sweetheart. He's so good with Isla, and he's been so lovely to me this past week. You two are pretty great together,' she said, brushing a strand of hair from her face. 'You think you'll ever get married or have kids or anything?'

Jake frowned at her. That was the second time in a week someone had asked him that. 'Maybe,' he admitted. 'The marriage anyway. Don't know about the kids. Maybe one will be enough for me?'

'What about Danny? You think he wants any? He seems to love them.' Jake smiled. Danny did love kids and was a big one himself.

'I dunno,' Jake confessed. 'What about you?'

Siobhan looked down at her stomach. 'Well, I'll be having another one in five months.'

'I mean get married again. Would you?'

'I'd like to, but I think I just want to focus on the girls for a while, you know?'

'Girls?' Jake flashed an eyebrow at her.

'Oh yeah,' she blushed again. 'I found out the sex. Another girl.'

'Cool.'

'Hmm. Two kids, though? On my own.' She shook her head.

'You're not on your own,' he reminded her.

'Oh, I'm sorry, I know you're always there for Isla.'

Jake stared at her. She looked so lost that it tugged at his heartstrings, and there was a time when he'd wondered if he even had one of those. He loved this woman and he would never see her struggle. He could hardly believe what he was about to propose. Danny might not be happy about it, but he would understand that family are the most important thing and they have to come first.

Danny was on his way into the kitchen when he heard the familiar voices of Siobhan and Jake.

'So, you honestly think we can make this work then?' Siobhan asked. Danny stopped in his tracks and listened.

'Yeah, I think we can.'

'Even with everything that's happened between us in the past?'

'Yeah. You know I love you, Siobhan.'

Danny's heart stopped beating. He knew he shouldn't eavesdrop, but how could he walk into that room now, and how could he walk away?

'I know you love me even if you hate me sometimes,' Jake went on. There was more laughter from Siobhan before Jake carried on. 'And we both love Isla. We only want what's best for her, don't we? We can make this work.'

'But what about Danny?' she asked.

Yeah, Jake, what about me? Danny thought to himself.

'Leave Danny to me. I'll take care of it.'

The sound of the front door opening startled him. He had to get out of the hallway before somebody saw him, and he couldn't go into the kitchen because he couldn't face the two of them. He turned and bolted for the stairs, running up them until he was in the bedroom that he and Jake shared when they stayed over.

Closing the door, he leaned back against it and took deep breaths as he looked around the room. His and Jake's stuff was scattered everywhere and it made his chest ache to think how easily they had slotted into each other's lives and how it could all just fade away. Sometimes it felt like they'd known each other for ever. He should have known happiness like that never lasted.

Chapter Thirty-Three

Danny was staring out of the window when he heard the bedroom door opening behind him. He sucked in a shaky breath and turned around, his eyes locking with Jake's. The look on his face told him they were about to have a conversation that would change both of their lives. He should distract him. He should try to prevent it from happening, but wasn't that just delaying the inevitable?

Maybe he should consider a pre-emptive strike? Tell Jake the last few months had been fun, but that's all it was. It was over now and they could both go back to their regular lives? Then at least he might get to walk out of there with some dignity.

'Can we talk?' Jake said and then it was too late. He'd said those terror-inducing words and so they would have to talk. And no matter how much Danny might want to protect his ego, he couldn't lie to this man whom he loved more than anyone in the world, and pretend that he didn't.

Instead he took another deep breath and walked toward him. 'Yeah. What about?' he asked, his voice cracking with emotion. He couldn't stop thinking about the fact that just a week ago, they had been planning on buying a fucking house together and now they were over. Just like that.

'I have something to ask you,' Jake said softly. 'Well, two things actually.'

'Okay?' Danny frowned at him.

'But first I wanted to thank you for this past week. You've been amazing, Dan. I couldn't have got through it without you. I know I've spent a lot of time with Siobhan. I'm sorry if I've neglected you.'

'Well, your daughter was missing, Jake. You and she were the only ones who knew what each other was going through,' Danny said with a shrug, trying to play the emotion of the whole week down as much as possible. Because if he cried when Jake Conlon broke his heart, he'd never be able to look him in the eye again.

'Yeah, but you understood exactly what I needed, Dan. You are always there for me…' He stopped speaking and shook his head. 'Fuck, why is this so fucking hard?'

'Just say it. Say whatever it is you came here to say, so we can both move forward,' Danny snapped.

'Okay,' Jake said with a frown. 'I wanted to ask you…' He stopped again and licked his lips.

'What?' Danny whispered as his heart stopped beating in his chest.

'Will you marry me, Dan?' He said it clearly enough, but despite that Danny was sure he'd misheard him.

'What?'

'I want to marry you, Dan. I know you're still figuring yourself out and shit, but figure yourself out with me.'

Danny opened and closed his mouth like a fish out of water while his brain caught up with him. 'But I thought you and Siobhan were…' He shook his head as confusion clouded his brain. He'd been completely prepared for one kind of conversation and was now faced with an entirely different one. One that he hadn't expected in the least.

'Me and Siobhan were what?' Jake frowned at him.

'I thought you were getting closer, and maybe… I dunno.' Danny shook his head. How did he tell him that he'd just been listening in on his private conversation with his ex-wife?

'Fuck no! That is the last thing I want. It's the last thing she wants. I'll always love her, Dan. She'll always be part of my life, but not like that. Nothing like what I feel about you. But Siobhan and Isla are kind of my second question.'

'And that is?'

'You haven't answered my first one yet,' Jake reminded him, his handsome features twisted into a scowl.

'Oh.' He'd never thought about marrying anyone and definitely not another man.

'Fucking hell, Dan. You're killing me,' Jake said as he shifted from one foot to the other.

'You really want to marry me? Me and you? Like for ever?'

'Yes, fucking for ever, soft lad. Can you answer the fucking question?'

Danny smiled. 'Yeah, course I'll marry you.'

Jake's face broke into a huge grin. Danny resisted the urge to kiss him, because he needed to know what else Jake wanted to ask him. 'What was the second question?'

Jake sucked in a breath. 'If we buy that big house, what do you think about Isla and Siobhan living with us?'

'What?' Danny blinked at him. He liked Siobhan but she was Jake's ex-wife.

'And not just them two. She's pregnant.'

'Pregnant?' Danny stared at him. 'Is it yours?'

'For fuck's sake! Of course not. You think I'd ask you to marry me and then confess to cheating with my ex-wife?'

'No,' Danny admitted.

'It's a long story. The real dad is out of the picture. She doesn't want to be on her own with two kids. She'll meet someone herself one day, but she hates living on her own. And Isla will be with us all full time. There's that room over the garage and the extension. We could make it a little bit self-contained for her so that we could all have our own privacy? I know it's a lot, Dan, and I don't mind if you say no.'

'You don't?' Danny asked with a frown, not quite believing him, because Jake was used to getting his own way about everything.

'No. Honest. Now that you've said yes to my first question, you can pretty much walk all over me for the rest of my life,' he said with a grin as he wrapped his arms around Danny's waist.

'Oh, I can?' Danny grinned back.

'Yeah.'

'Good to know, and I'll think about Siobhan. Okay?' Danny said. It would be nice having Isla living with them and even the thought of a new baby made him smile. Danny had realised lately that he loved kids, and he did like Siobhan, as long as she had no ideas about her and Jake getting back together.

'Okay,' Jake said. 'Now are we gonna pack our shit up and get back to our own place, because I miss you walking around in just your boxers.' He kissed Danny's neck and murmured, 'But not as much as I miss being able to do that thing that makes you scream.'

'I do not fucking scream,' Danny insisted.

'Okay. You shout in a high-pitched voice, then. I miss that.' Jake chuckled as he peppered kisses over his fiancé's throat.

'I think you'll find that I roar. Like a lion.' Danny laughed too.

'Like a fucking pussycat.'

'Whatever, smart-arse. But you're going to need to soundproof our room in this new house then, aren't you?'

'Already thought about that.'

Chapter Thirty-Four

Kevin Grosvenor looked up at the huge steel gates of Nudge Richards' scrapyard. They were open, so he took the opportunity to drive inside. Parking up his new Volkswagen, he climbed out and made his way to the small Portakabin that Nudge used as an office.

The door was closed, so he knocked. No need to piss the man off before he needed to.

'Come in,' a voice bellowed. He recognised it, but it didn't belong to Nudge.

He pushed it open with a loud creak and blinked when he saw Danny Alexander and Luke Sullivan sitting inside. What the hell were those two doing there? He'd had enough of their family to last him a lifetime. Isla Conlon had apparently been returned to Grace Carter's house – as if by magic. Completely unharmed, fortunately. A woman named Sandra Redman had been responsible for taking her. That same woman had been found dead in her flat just an hour later. It appeared to be suicide. She had never had a drug problem that was known about, but she had injected herself with medical-grade morphine. He didn't for a minute believe she'd done it herself, but he had no way of proving otherwise. There was no trace of forced entry and no evidence of anyone else at the scene.

Danny had his feet up on the desk and was glancing through some paperwork, while Luke was sitting at the desk with a laptop open in front of him.

They both looked up when he walked into the room.

'What can we do for you, Detective Inspector?' Danny asked with a frown.

'I'm looking for Nudge.'

'He doesn't work here anymore,' Luke replied.

'Since when?' Kevin asked. That was the first he'd heard of it.

'Last week,' Luke replied with a shrug.

'So where is he?'

'Retired,' Danny replied. 'Finally fucked off to the Costa Del Sol like he'd always planned.'

Kevin looked around the room. It was certainly cleaner and tidier than the place had ever been with Nudge around. In fact, everything looked to be brand new. What the fuck were these two hiding?

'Just like that?' Kevin asked as he stepped further inside.

'Well, he's been planning it for a while, but I doubt he'd have shared his plans with you and your colleagues, Detective,' Luke said with a smile.

'Sold the place to you then?'

'Nope.' Danny shook his head. 'It's been our place for years.'

'What?' Kevin shook his head in confusion. 'Nudge has had this place for ever.'

'I think you'll find he sold it some years ago,' Danny said as he took his feet from the table and sat up straighter. Suddenly, the atmosphere in the room was getting a little less friendly.

'To who?'

'Grace Carter,' Danny replied.

'Oh, so it's your boyfriend's mum's place then, is it? Not yours?' He smirked, trying to push a button. He knew these two were hiding something and he wanted to know what that was. He needed Nudge to help with the passport for Milo Savage, because he needed him and John Barrow off his back so he could fucking breathe again. He noticed the look of warning that Luke shot his business partner. He had always been the more reasonable of the two.

'My future mother-in-law's place, actually.' Danny smirked right back. 'And she's all about her family being owners in the business. So, yeah, it's ours too, right, Luke?'

'Right,' Luke nodded.

'Fuck!' Kevin said as he ran a hand over his jaw.

'Anything we can help you with, Detective?' Danny asked.

He stared at them both. He was desperate, but he couldn't ask these two about false passports. He could have manipulated Nudge, handled him so that he'd have kept his mouth shut, but he would have no such luck with

Danny and Luke. If they helped him, he would be on their hook for ever. But he could ask questions.

'Either of you know a guy by the name of Milo Savage?' he asked. The tension that burst into the room and into their shoulders told him that they did, and that their connection wasn't a positive one.

'Why?' Luke asked.

'I'm working a case and his name came up,' he said, deciding to bait the hook and see if he caught anything. 'I'm going to speak to him and I just wondered if you'd had any dealings with him. Sounds like a piece of shit.'

'He is. You know where he is?' Danny asked.

Bingo! 'I have a lead to follow,' Kevin replied.

Danny and Luke looked at each other but said nothing more. But that didn't matter to Kevin. Milo Savage was obviously not their favourite person and he could use that to his advantage, he was sure of it.

As soon as he climbed into his car, DI Grosvenor dialled John Barrow's number.

'What the fuck is it now, Kevin?' he said with a dramatic sigh.

Kevin smiled. He would love nothing more than to have this arrogant piece of shit removed from the face of the earth. But he had to make sure he had all bases covered. He had to confirm that his suspicions were right, because if they were, he could take out both threats at once.

'I just wanted you to know that I'm sorting the passport, but before I meet with this prick, who is he running from, John?'

'You don't need to know that,' he replied dismissively.

'The fuck I don't. If whoever it is finds out that I helped him, then me and my family are in the firing line too. What's it to you if I know who he fucked over?'

Barrow laughed sarcastically. 'I thought you'd have figured it out already, to be honest, Detective Inspector.'

'Well, I have my suspicions,' he replied.

'And they are?'

'The Carters?'

'Who else?' Barrow laughed again. 'They won't be around for much longer though, will they?'

'Won't they?'

'You did go to Nudge Richards for the passport? I told you you'd need a good fence.'

The hairs on the back of his neck stood on end and every instinct he'd carefully honed over the years told him that he was being played in more ways than he already knew. 'You did tell me that, but I went elsewhere.'

'You didn't go to Nudge?'

'No.'

'But I heard you had a big case. One involving the Carters?'

'Fuck me, you are out of the loop, John. That was a kidnapping. Somebody took Jake Conlon's daughter.'

'So you didn't go to see Nudge?' Barrow snapped, the

frustration evident in his tone now rather than his earlier sarcasm.

'No. Why would you think that he was anything to do with my case?'

'For fuck's sake, Kevin,' he snarled. 'Must I hold your hand through every single thing? I have handed you the keys to bring down those arrogant bastards once and for all. Go to Nudge Richards' scrapyard and do your job.'

'What will I find there, John?' he asked, already knowing the answer. Absolutely nothing because the Carters were in control of the place now and whatever might have been there was now long gone. Nudge was a friend of theirs. A loyal soldier of Grace Carter and one of her trusted inner circle. He didn't believe for a second they had made him disappear on purpose. So what the fuck had Barrow expected him to find there when he'd pointed him in that direction? What might Kevin have found if he'd gone there that day when Isla Conlon went missing?

'You'll find years of evidence of the Carters and Conlon using that place to cover up their crimes. You'll have enough on all of them – Michael, Sean, Connor, Jake – even that oaf John Brennan.'

'But I can't just go in and look for that stuff,' Kevin replied, acting naïve. He knew exactly what Barrow was getting at, but he wanted to hear him say it.

'God, you really are thick, Kevin,' he spat. 'I've given you a reason to go over the place with a fine-tooth comb. You can thank me later.' Then he ended the call and Kevin shook his head. So Nudge hadn't retired to the Costa del Sol after all. Barrow had had him killed so that Kevin would find the dead body and open a murder investigation – and even if there was no evidence of the Carters being involved in Nudge's death, Kevin would find evidence to connect them to plenty of other crimes instead. Kevin had to admit, it was a pretty good plan, even if he did feel like he'd been used as a puppet. Well, Barrow would pull his strings no longer.

Kevin dialled Milo Savage's number next.

'You'd better have some good news for me,' he snarled when he answered.

'I do actually,' he replied. He couldn't wait to get rid of this piece of shit either. 'I found someone to sort the passport.'

'About fucking time,' Milo snapped.

'Yeah, sorry it took a while.'

'When can you get it me by?'

'Two or three days,' he replied. Any sooner and Milo might get suspicious. 'And you'll need to send me a picture.'

'Yeah. I can do that,' he said, his tone slightly calmer.

'Good. Send it to this number and I'll be in touch when it's ready.'

Milo didn't speak again. The line went dead and Kevin was left holding his phone against his ear. But at least now he knew exactly what he needed to do.

Chapter Thirty-Five

Connor Carter was admiring his wife's arse in her new dress as she was making lunch, and contemplating taking her to bed for the afternoon, when the buzzer rang to signal someone was at the front gate.

He sighed as he went to open it. Their son was with his dad and Grace for the afternoon and they weren't expecting visitors. He walked to the security monitor and looked at the screen.

'Who is it?' Jazz asked with a frown.

'It's that fucking detective,' Connor snarled.

'What does he want?'

'Let's find out,' he said as he pressed the button to allow him to speak through the intercom. 'What can I do for you, Detective?'

'Mr Carter, I need to discuss something with you. Can I come in?'

'Discuss what?' Connor snapped, immediately suspicious of anything to do with the police.

'It's regarding a mutual acquaintance of ours, Milo Savage. I believe I can arrange a meeting with him, if that's something you're interested in?'

Connor took his finger off the button so he could speak to his wife in private.

'You think he's being serious?' he asked her.

'No idea. But he obviously knows we're looking for him. It can't hurt to hear what he has to say.'

'Hmm. And we already suspected he wasn't completely straight because of the way he handled the whole investigation into Danny's mum's murder,' Connor said. 'I don't trust him even a little bit.'

Jazz ran her fingertips over his cheek. 'You don't have to trust him, baby, just hear him out. If there is a chance he could lead us to Milo, then we should take it.'

Connor nodded his agreement and then pressed the button to open the electronic gates. He watched on the screen as Detective Inspector Grosvenor drove in and parked up on the driveway. His interest was well and truly piqued.

A few minutes later, Grosvenor was sitting in Connor and Jasmine's kitchen.

'Shall we get straight to the point, Detective?' Connor said as he sat opposite him. 'This is supposed to be my quiet time with my wife and you're interrupting it, so no bullshit. Okay?'

Grosvenor nodded. 'I can arrange a meeting with Milo Savage.'

Connor crossed his arms over his chest. 'And why would I care about that?'

'This "no bullshit" thing cuts both ways, Mr Carter. I know he's on the run and I know it's you he's running from.'

'And how do you know that?'

'Because I'm the man who's been asked to help get him out of the country.'

Connor narrowed his eyes at him, staring him down and wondering what the hell his angle was, when Jazz spoke. 'Why you?'

'He's blackmailing me. At least a friend of his is. Former Chief Superintendent John Barrow. I believe you know him too?'

'Doesn't everyone?' Connor snapped.

'I suppose,' Grosvenor replied.

'So, you expect me to do your dirty work for you or something? Do you think I'm a mug? Is this some kind of set-up?'

'No.' Kevin shook his head vehemently. 'I want both of them out of my life, I'm not going to deny that, but I know that you do too. I'm risking my job here.'

'Well, Milo I'd love to see the back of, but I'm not that arsed about some nonce ex-copper,' Connor replied with a shrug.

'You should be…'

'Is that a threat?' Connor snarled as he pushed back his chair and stood, towering over the detective.

'No. But he has it in for you and your family. He is determined to take you down. It was him who was behind the idea to frame you, or Danny, for Glenda Alexander's murder.'

'The investigation you handled?' Connor said, his eyes burning into Grosvenor's. The detective visibly blanched. He knew he was heading into dangerous territory.

'Yes.' Grosvenor swallowed. 'But not just that. He had Nudge Richards killed too, so that we'd have a reason to tear the place apart and maybe find some evidence of possible crimes that you or your family may have been involved in.'

'Nudge?' Connor said quietly as he sat back down again and Jazz put a hand on his shoulder.

'Yeah. I was supposed to find him and open an investigation.'

'And what will you do now?' Jasmine asked.

'Nothing. Nudge has retired, right? Gone to live in the Costa Del Sol?'

'Where is Milo?' Connor snapped.

'I don't know, but I have his number and I'm supposed to arrange to drop off a passport to him in a few days. You pick the time and place and I'll tell him.'

'If this is some sort of fucking trap…' Connor warned.

'It's not. I swear.'

Connor narrowed his eyes at him, considering whether

he was telling the truth. Grosvenor was a snake, just like the rest of them, but he did believe the man was there to save his own skin, and luckily for him they had a common enemy. Both Barrow and Savage would be dead before the week was out.

As soon as Grosvenor had left, Connor called Jake to bring him up to speed.

'Fuck! So Nudge was killed just so they could get some dirt on us. What the fuck does this piece of shit Barrow have against us, anyway?' Jake asked.

'Probably pissed off he could never put us away,' Connor replied. 'So we arrange the meeting with Savage, but what about Barrow? How do we deal with him?'

'I know just the man. Leave it with me.'

Chapter Thirty-Six

J ake walked up the steps of the Portakabin in Nudge Richards' scrapyard. He shook his head as he remembered he'd have to stop calling it that. It was his family's place now and poor Nudge was six feet under. He could hardly believe that cunt Barrow had it in for his family so bad that he had someone murdered just so the bizzies would look into this place. Well, no matter what happened now, they had made sure there was no evidence of any of their crimes anywhere. The old containers that they'd used had been forensically cleaned – Connor was an expert on that shit – and Danny had thrown himself into the task of sprucing the place up. It had given him something to focus on in the past week, and for that Jake was grateful. Danny hated dirt and grime and he refused to work every day in a place that made his skin crawl.

Jake pushed open the wooden door and looked around the makeshift office. Danny's effect on the place was most evident in here. It had been a dump when Nudge had been resident. In fact it was a long-standing joke that accepting a mug of tea from Nudge was a lottery – you might get a nice brew, or you might just get dysentery.

Danny had gutted the place, scrubbed it clean and then burned everything – except for the Constable knock-off, which he'd kept in memory of their old acquaintance – before replacing it with new stuff. It was a pretty nice-looking pad now, and he could see why Luke and Danny were keen to make more of this part of the business. Scrap metal was a nice earner. After everything that had happened in the past week, Jake had taken more of an interest in their legitimate companies. Once they had sorted out the whole Milo Savage and Barrow situation, he had a feeling that a conversation with Connor about the future of their business was on the cards.

'Jake?' Danny said with a smile as he noticed him walking into the room. 'What are you doing here?'

'I wanted to see what you two had done with the place. Fuck me.' He whistled as he looked around. 'I don't recognise it. It's like Nudge was never here.'

'We kept his Constable,' Luke said with a grin as he nodded toward the ugly painting hanging above the small kitchenette area.

'Yeah, well, he'd have haunted you if you'd have binned that. Do you know he swore it was real?'

'Maybe it is,' Danny said with a shrug. 'Not like any of us would know the difference.'

'Are you kidding?' Jake laughed as he took a seat on one

of the plush new office chairs. 'If Nudge had a real Constable, he'd have flogged it a long time ago.'

'Maybe not.' Danny shook his head. 'He said it was his grandad's. Maybe it had some sentimental value?'

Jake looked at the painting again. It was ugly as fuck and not his cup of tea at all, but he doubted that Nudge Richards had had a priceless piece of art hanging in his shit-box Portakabin all these years.

'You just come here to pick up your fiancé, then?' Luke asked with a grin.

'Fuck off, knobhead,' Danny snapped as his face turned red and Jake started to laugh.

Luke ruffled Danny's hair. 'I'm only messing with you, soft lad.' Then he turned to Jake. 'Congratulations, by the way.'

'Thanks, mate. And I did come here to pick up my future husband, but I wanted to fill you in on some stuff too. After Detective Grosvenor paid you two a visit, he went to see Connor too.'

'Connor? What for?' Danny asked with a frown.

Jake filled them in on what Grosvenor had told Connor and they both sat staring at him in surprise until he finished speaking.

'Fuck! That Barrow is a cunt,' Luke snarled.

'So is Grosvenor,' Danny added with a scowl. 'I'd like to slit that fucker's throat too.'

Jake shook his head. 'We leave him out of it. I know he fucked us over, but he's doing us a favour now, and it won't hurt to have something over him in the future, will it? We already know he's as bent as a nine-bob note. He's got kids as well, Dan. Young kids.'

Danny shook his head in annoyance and crossed his arms over his chest but Jake knew he agreed with him really.

'You're not mellowing, are you, Jake?' Luke asked.

'You know, I think I am.' He started to laugh.

'So you and Connor are meeting with Milo Savage. How are we gonna sort out this prick Barrow, though?'

'Well, we want you two with us when we meet Savage, and—' He was interrupted by his mobile ringing. Taking it out of his pocket he smiled at the number on the screen. 'Here is the solution to our other problem right now.'

Jake pressed the phone to his ear. 'Dave. Thanks for getting back to me.' Dave was a prison officer in HMP Strangeways and he was always open to earning a few extra quid where and when he could.

'No problem. I have him here. You got about two minutes. Okay?'

'Two minutes is all I need.'

He heard the muffled sound of voices before the phone was passed.

'Jake?'

'Craig. How is prison life treating you? Good, I assume?' Jake asked. Craig Johnson and his brothers had crossed him and his family and three of them had paid with their lives. The only reason that Craig and his brother Ged were still breathing was because they had murdered one of their brothers in reparation. For that, and because it had got Jake and Connor out of prison for a murder that they *had* actually committed, they gave Craig and Ged their protection.

'Can't complain,' he replied.

'I need to call in that favour you owe me.'

'I already paid my debt,' Craig snapped.

'Nah,' Jake said. 'Not even close, mate. But do this and you'll be free and clear. Promise.'

'How do I know you'll keep your word?'

'Because unlike you, Craig, I am a man of my word. I never told you your debt was repaid. You did what you did to save yourself and your only surviving brother. This is to clear your debt. Besides, you're going to enjoy this. I know it. Play your cards right and you'll be the king of the entire fucking prison.'

'What is it?'

'John Barrow,' Jake replied.

'The nonce copper?'

'Former copper,' Jake reminded him.

'Former or not, he's under constant watch, Jake. If not, he'd have been well done in by now.'

'Well, that's where my mate Dave is going to help, you see. He'll create an opportunity and all you need to do is take it.'

'And if I don't?'

'Then your time in there is going to get a whole lot more uncomfortable, Craig. Think not-being-able-to-sit-down uncomfortable.'

'Fuck!' Craig muttered. 'If I do this, we're done? I'm safe? Ged is safe? My family are safe?'

'Scout's honour.'

There was a few seconds' pause before he replied. 'Okay.'

'Good lad. Dave will let you know where and when.' Jake ended the call and placed his phone back in his pocket.

'Was that Craig Johnson?' Luke asked.

'The one and only,' Jake replied.

Danny frowned at him. 'You're going to trust that snake with this?'

'He killed his own brother to save his skin. I'm pretty sure he's capable of killing Barrow. And if he doesn't, I'll find someone else who will, and it will also give me an excuse to take out the Johnson brothers too.'

'Smart move then. You have any idea when it's going to happen?' Luke asked.

'I told Dave I need it to happen in two days. He's never let me down before. Once Barrow finds out that Savage is out of the picture, he might get suspicious and demand a move. He might even have the clout to orchestrate one himself. And vice versa – if Barrow is taken out, then Savage might get twitchy. And we don't know how much contact they have with each other, so I'd prefer both of them gone around the same time.'

'That makes sense,' Danny agreed.

'Did Danny just agree with me?' Jake arched an eyebrow at Luke, who smiled and shook his head.

'I agree with you all the time,' Danny protested.

'No. You question every single fucking thing I say,' Jake said with a smile.

'You do,' Luke agreed. 'You get away with it though, so don't worry. Someone needs to keep this cocky fucker in line.'

Jake narrowed his eyes at Luke. 'If you weren't my uncle…' he said, but there was no menace in his tone.

'Yeah, right,' Luke said as he stood. 'Shall we get the fuck out of here and grab something to eat?'

'Yes,' Danny declared, thankful for the change of subject. 'Let's call Stacey too.'

Chapter Thirty-Seven

John Barrow walked down the hallway behind the prison officer, Dave. He liked Dave. He was a man who was open to manipulation and bribery, and that was his favourite kind of person. He had an unexpected legal visit this morning. He hadn't been told about it, but then his solicitor was beyond useless half the time. He'd fucked up his shot at an appeal and had claimed that Barrow had no grounds – the man was an imbecile. But perhaps he'd have better news for him today. He smiled to himself as he followed Dave through an unfamiliar door.

'Are you sure this is the right way?' he asked as he glanced around his surroundings.

'Short cut,' Dave replied nonchalantly and suddenly Barrow had a strange feeling settling in the pit of his stomach.

'Actually, I don't want to see my brief today,' he said as Dave turned to look at him. 'Feeling a bit queasy,' he said as he rubbed a hand over his stomach. He was probably being paranoid, but better safe than sorry.

'We're almost there,' Dave said with a smile.

'No. I want to go back to my pad.' Barrow turned on his heel only to come face to face with another prison officer. He was a mountain of a man with a ginger beard and eyes the colour of whisky.

'I don't think that's going to happen, Mr Barrow,' the screw said with a sneer. *Oh, fuck.* This was one of those high and mighty types who looked down their noses at people like him. He backed up, searching for the safety of Dave, who would look after him, surely? But when he turned around again, searching for the familiar friendly face, another prisoner was standing there instead.

'All right,' he said in a thick Scouse accent. 'Going somewhere?'

But even in the face of certain defeat, Barrow couldn't shake the arrogance and entitlement that had been bred into him the moment he was born. Always convinced that he was the better man and that someone would step in and save him, because that was how it had gone all his life. But not today.

He sneered at the man in front of him. *Peasant!*

'Out of m—' he sputtered as the blade was plunged into his stomach.

'Mr Conlon and Mr Carter send their warmest regards,' his attacker hissed as he brought his face so close to Barrow's that he could see himself reflected in the man's dark eyes. He wasn't sure what had happened. He didn't feel any pain at first, just warmth spreading through his abdomen.

'You'd better make sure he doesn't get back up,' Dave said from somewhere behind the man who had just stabbed him.

'My fucking pleasure,' he snarled as he drove the knife in again. This time, Barrow felt the searing pain burning through him. He dropped to his knees.

'Rot in hell, you sick fuck!' the prisoner snarled and then he spat on him. He actually spat on him. Barrow lay on the floor, blood pumping out of the wounds in his stomach and someone else's saliva running down his face. Until his very last breath, he remained convinced that someone would save him.

Chapter Thirty-Eight

J ake frowned at Detective Inspector Grosvenor as he sat on a stool at the breakfast bar in Connor's kitchen, holding a mug of tea in his hands and looking a little too comfortable for Jake's liking – as though he were a welcome guest rather than a means to an end. Connor and Jazz sat beside him on one side of the island and Grosvenor sat opposite as though he was being interviewed. Jake smiled at the irony of the situation. Not so long ago, this piece of shit had tried to stitch Danny up for a murder he didn't commit. The least he could do was squirm a little.

'So call him and let's get this thing set up so we can get on with our day, yeah?' Connor said.

'Of course,' Grosvenor said, taking his phone out of his pocket. 'Tomorrow, right?'

'Yep. Try and make it somewhere quiet.'

'He made it clear he wants to choose the place. Is that

okay? I mean, I'd have no reason to pick a particular spot, and we don't want him to know he's being set up.'

'He can pick the place,' Connor snapped. 'Just fucking call him.'

Grosvenor nodded and unlocked his phone. 'I'm almost sorry I'm not going to see the look on his face when you turn up instead of me.'

Jake and Connor shared a glance before Connor put his hand over Grosvenor's, covering it completely and stopping him from using the phone. Grosvenor looked up with a frown.

'You are meeting him, soft-shite,' Connor snapped and Jake grinned. Now the squirming would begin.

'What?' Grosvenor said. He stared, open-mouthed, and pulled at his shirt collar with his free hand.

'You're meeting Savage.' Jake repeated it for him, louder this time.

'B-but I thought you were taking care of that?' he stammered.

'Nope,' Connor replied with a shake of his head. 'You think we're going to do all of your dirty work for you, Detective? You don't get off that lightly.'

Grosvenor swallowed, his discomfort obvious now. 'I thought I was only setting up the meeting?'

'Nope. We can't have your mate Milo getting spooked at the last minute, can we? We need you to make the handover, distract him and let him think he's won...'

'And then we'll take him,' Jake added.

'Yeah, it's always a bit sweeter when they already they think they won,' Connor said.

'Yup, you're boots on the ground for this one, Grosvenor,' Jake said with a grin. 'No sitting behind a desk and letting everyone else do the hard work when you work for us.'

'With us,' Connor said with a wink.

'Oh, yeah, with us.' Jake laughed as Grosvenor almost melted off the stool.

Connor released his grip on Grosvenor's hand and the detective regained his composure. A bead of sweat rolled down his forehead and he brushed it away before scrolling through his contacts and dialling a number. He held the phone to his ear and waited for the call to be answered. Jake watched his face intently. He hoped the man had it in him to be calm under pressure. Surely, given his job, he had to?

A few seconds later, the call was answered and they could hear the man speaking on the other end. 'You got what I need yet?' he barked.

'Yes.'

'About fucking time. Meet me in an hour.'

Grosvenor looked at Connor, who shook his head. There were things that needed to be put in place before they took Savage. It had to be done right.

'I can't. I don't actually have it right now, but I'm picking it up later tonight. How about we meet tomorrow morning?'

'You better not be setting me up, Grosvenor,' he snarled.

'I'm not. You came to me, remember? I just want this

done. Trust me, I want this dealt with just as quickly as you do.'

There was silence on the other end.

'Look, do you want this passport or not? You're only wanted on a recall for breaching your licence – who do you think I'm going to bring with me? Fucking Interpol?'

'Tomorrow morning. First thing?'

'First thing,' Grosvenor agreed.

'There's a café called Greedy's on Yardsley Road. Just outside Stoke. Meet me there at eight.'

'I want somewhere quiet,' Grosvenor said.

'It's quiet enough.'

Then the line went dead.

Jazz flipped her MacBook open and pulled up the place Milo had just mentioned. Clicking on the street view, she turned the screen to show the three men.

'Looks like a shit-hole,' Jake snapped.

'Move the screen around, babe, let's see what's round there,' Connor said.

Jazz did as he asked, moving the cursor so the camera panned around the street. There were a few more shops dotted along the road: a barber's and a pizza takeaway as well as what looked like a mobile phone repair shop. The rest of the shops looked to be boarded up.

'A two-way street,' Jake observed.

'Yeah,' Connor agreed as he peered at the screen. There were a few parked cars at one end of the street and he pointed to them. 'We can park up here and wait. Then as soon as he shows his face...'

'What, we drive past and grab him? Or easier to grab him in the café?'

'You know him better than any of us, babe.' Connor turned to his wife. 'Is he likely to make a scene?'

'As soon as he sees you, he'll know that his hours are numbered, and he will do anything he can to save his own skin.'

'We'll grab him in the café then,' Connor decided.

'How do I get him into the café? What if he doesn't want to go in there?' Grosvenor asked.

'You have something he needs. I'm sure you can think of a way,' Jake replied.

'We'll speak in the morning then, Detective,' Connor said as he stood up, indicating that Grosvenor's presence was no longer needed.

As soon as Connor returned to the room, Jazz said, 'You can't know who else is going to be in that café.'

'We know that, babe,' he said with a smile. 'That's why we're just going to drag him into the Land Rover.'

'But you just said…'

'If Grosvenor is going to fuck us over then it's best he doesn't know our entire plan,' Jake replied.

'I see,' Jazz said with an answering smile. 'I should never have doubted you.' She wrapped her arms around her husband's neck and gave him a kiss on the cheek.

Chapter Thirty-Nine

Connor killed the Land Rover's ignition and leaned back in his seat. He cracked his knuckles and the sound reverberated around the quiet car. Jake was sitting in the passenger seat beside him and Danny and Luke were in the back. They sat quietly watching the entrance to the greasy spoon from their vantage point a few hundred yards down the street. The car's blacked-out windows hid them from any prying eyes outside.

Grosvenor was going to do the handover to make sure that Milo didn't get spooked and run.

Danny looked out of the window at the dismal surroundings. 'No wonder we couldn't find the cunt,' he muttered. 'Who the fuck would hide out in a shit-hole like this?'

'Someone who didn't want to be found, numb-nuts,' Luke said with a grin.

Danny pulled a face at him.

'Perfect spot for a meeting like this anyway. I doubt anyone round here takes much notice of anything that goes on,' Connor said as he looked at the pale, stoned faces of two young men in their early twenties passing by. They could see why Savage had insisted on picking this spot for the meeting. He'd wanted a public place, but nowhere too public where someone might recognise him. It was the kind of place where so much shady shit went down that nobody paid any attention to anyone. A steady stream of cars passed up and down the street, some stopping at the vape shop, which they had all agreed must also be selling weed because people popped in and out of there too quickly for anything else.

'You think he's gonna show?' Jake asked.

'Has no reason not to. Unless Grosvenor has lost his nerve and spooked him somehow.'

Danny leaned forward in his seat, his hand on Connor's shoulder, and peered through the windscreen as Grosvenor casually read the menu taped to the window. 'I dunno, he doesn't look spooked to me. Seems like this kind of shady shit is right up his street.'

'Hmm. Bent fucker,' Jake muttered.

'Do you know what this Milo cunt looks like?' Luke asked. 'I mean, he might walk right past us on his way to Grosvenor.'

'Me and Jake looked up an old picture of him on Google from when he was sent down, and Jazz said he hasn't changed much, so yeah.'

'Here he comes.' Jake nodded toward the figure dressed

A Score to Settle

in a dark tracksuit heading toward the spot where Grosvenor was standing. His hair was longer now and he had a beard, but it was undeniably Milo Savage.

'Let's go then,' Connor snarled as he pulled away from the kerb and crawled along the road.

A few seconds later the car rolled to a stop beside DI Kevin Grosvenor and Milo Savage. The latter didn't know what had hit him when he was grabbed in a firm headlock and manhandled into the back of a car.

'What the fuck?' he spat as he struggled in Danny's grip, but his strength was no match for Danny's, especially when Luke grabbed hold of Milo's arm and yanked him further into the vehicle, which then sped off before Danny had even had a chance to close the door. Once he had, Danny shoved Milo back against the seat between him and Luke. Savage tried to punch him.

'I will fucking knock you out if you don't sit still, you cunt,' Danny snarled.

'Who the fuck do you think you are?' Milo snarled back.

'Surely you know exactly who we are, mate?' Connor said, eyeing their hostage in the rear-view mirror.

Milo shrugged Danny's hand off his shoulder and stared back at him. The man who had stolen the woman he loved. The man he'd tried to frame for murder. He swallowed as the realisation of what was about to happen hit him like a sledgehammer to the gut. That probably meant that one of the other men in this car was the man he'd *actually* framed for murder. Fuck! He was done for.

Milo quickly glanced at the two men sitting on either

side of him, who had him literally pinned between their huge bodies. Milo could hold his own in a fight if he needed to, but it had never really been his area of expertise. He preferred to leave that to the people working for him. He prided himself on being the brains of any operations. Even when he was Sol Shepherd's right-hand man, he'd been the strategist. His heart sank as he realised there was no strategising his way out of this one. He assumed if Connor Carter was driving, the good-looking fucker sitting in the passenger seat had to be Jake Conlon. Of course it was. He was the double of his old man Nathan. Milo had met him a few times back in the day. He'd been an arrogant prick and, if the rumours were true, the apple hadn't fallen far from the tree in that respect. He figured that must mean he was sitting between Luke Sullivan and Danny Alexander. He had no chance of escape while he was in this car.

A bead of sweat rolled down his forehead as the rumours of what Connor Carter liked to do to his enemies suddenly came back to him. His sphincter clenched and his stomach rolled as he fought the urge to throw up. That fucker Grosvenor had stitched him up. Cunt! He should have known never to trust a bent copper.

'Where the fuck are you taking me?' he asked, feigning bravado, because men like these thrived on fear and he wouldn't give them the satisfaction of knowing he was trying his best not to shit his pants.

'You don't need to worry about where we're going,' Connor Carter replied.

'All you need to know is that you won't be coming back

from there,' Jake added and the muscle-head to the right of him who had just dragged him into the car, chuckled to himself.

Milo sat back in the seat and his heart raced like he'd just been given a shot of pure adrenaline. For some reason he thought of the spy movies he used to watch when he was a kid, and how the captured enemy would snap off their false tooth and ingest a cyanide capsule rather than talk. As a person whose top priority in life had always been self-preservation, he could never understand why they would do that. But right now, sitting in the back of this car with four psychopaths who wanted to make him pay for crossing them, he would kill for such an out.

Chapter Forty

Connor Carter pulled off his hooded sweatshirt and tossed it onto a chair in the corner of the room. They'd driven half an hour to an empty warehouse on the outskirts of Liverpool which was one of the many buildings Cartel Securities protected.

Milo Savage was strung up on a huge metal hook by his wrists wearing nothing but his boxer shorts. He was hoisted so high that he had to stand on the tips of his toes to prevent the chains on his wrists from taking his full weight and cutting into him. Blood from a cut above his eye that he'd sustained when being removed from the car trickled down his face and onto his chest. He shivered in the cold room, but despite that, sweat beaded on his forehead.

'You got everything you need, Con?' Jake asked, scanning the equipment that he and Luke had carried in from the car.

'I think so,' Connor replied, running a hand over his

beard. 'That thing charged up?' He indicated the huge battery they had lugged in and left beside Milo's feet.

'Full of juice and ready to go,' Jake confirmed.

Connor started removing his T-shirt. Jake watched his best mate moving around the small space, his hands brushing over the tools they had laid out for him. He was no longer the same man who'd walked in five minutes earlier – he'd already gone to that space in his head that allowed him to do the shit he did. Jake had seen Connor Carter in action plenty of times. They had broken bones together, even beaten someone to death with their fists after Paul died, but he had never seen him at this level of psycho before. He would say he was feral if he didn't seem so calm and controlled.

'What the fuck are you planning on doing to me?' Milo spat. 'You sick fuck!'

'Says the man who used to buy and sell women like they were fucking dogs,' Luke snarled, giving Milo a punch in the gut that made him retch.

He gasped for air and when he looked up he saw Connor connecting a pair of jump cables to the battery on the floor beside him. His lip started to tremble and that was when he began to beg.

'Please. I have friends. I know people,' he snivelled. 'People who might be useful to you.'

'Like your mate John Barrow?' Jake laughed. 'Afraid he's had himself an unfortunate accident in prison, lad. Fell on a knife, so I heard.'

'W-what?' Milo stammered. 'No.'

'Yep,' Jake nodded.

'Did that cunt Grosvenor set me up?'

'What do you think, gobshite?' Danny snarled.

Connor didn't join in the conversation. He continued silently working away while Jake, Danny and Luke taunted their hostage.

When Connor was ready, he moved silently between his business partners and friends, standing directly in front of Milo, with a jump cable in each hand.

'Pour the water,' he ordered no one in particular.

Danny was nearest to the water bottles they'd brought in, so he picked one up and poured it over Milo's chest, ignoring him as he screamed and bucked on his chains. 'No! No!'

When Danny was done, he stepped back.

'How many times did you fuck my wife?' Connor snarled.

'What?' Milo spat.

'I said how many times did you fuck my wife?' Connor roared, pressing the cables to Milo's chest. The sound and smell of burning flesh forced Danny to cover his nose. He wanted Milo to suffer as much as anyone – he was the reason he'd done two weeks in Walton nick – but he couldn't abide the stench.

Jake looked at him and tilted his head towards the door. 'Come on. We can wait outside. He prefers to work alone anyway.' He looked at his best mate, who seemed completely oblivious to anyone but Milo.

'I'll wait in here in case he needs me,' Luke offered.

Jake patted his uncle on the back. 'Thanks, mate.'

Danny and Jake walked out of the warehouse and into the mid-afternoon sun. Danny sucked in a lungful of fresh air as he leaned against the wall.

'You all right there, tiger?' Jake asked with a grin.

'Yeah.' He took another deep breath. 'It was the smell. I couldn't...' He put his hand to his mouth as even the memory of it made him feel sick.

'He'll shit his pants soon, if Connor keeps that up, so probably a good job we got you out of there.'

'I've never seen him like that before. It was like he completely zoned out.'

'No, well, he doesn't get like that often, but when he does, best to keep out of his way and let him do his shit until he comes back down to earth.'

'Will Luke be okay?' Danny asked anxiously as he checked the door.

'Course he will. Connor is pissed off and he's in the zone. He hasn't completely lost his marbles, Dan. He still knows who we are.'

'Okay.' Danny took a packet of Polo mints out of his jacket pocket. 'Want one?' he asked before he popped three into his own mouth.

Jake took two from the packet and then the two of them stood there for an hour, listening to the screams of Milo Savage as Connor Carter tortured him to death.

Chapter Forty-One

M ichael Carter carried the bottle of brandy to the table while Grace took some crystal glasses from the cupboard. He looked at his two grown sons, Connor and Jake. The latter was technically his stepson, but he considered him as much a son as the three he had fathered. Jazz sat beside Connor, her hand resting on his thigh. Whenever they were near each other, they were usually touching and it made him smile. Jazz brought a sense of peace and happiness to his son's life and Michael would always be grateful to her for it.

Jake sat on the opposite side of the room in the armchair while Danny sat on its arm. The two of them were chatting about something and whatever it was made Danny bend and kiss the top of Jake's head. There had been a time when the lad had seemed terrified of any public displays of affection, and it was good to see that he was finally getting over whatever it was that had been holding him back from his commitment to Jake. The fact that the two of them were planning on getting married had made Grace unbelievably happy and so he was grateful for Danny's influence in their lives too.

'You need a hand there, sis?' Luke asked as he watched Grace stacking the crystal tumblers from his seat on one of the sofas next to Danny's sister, Stacey, who had her feet tucked beneath her as she leaned against his chest.

'No. I'm fine,' she replied with a smile as she carried all eight glasses effortlessly, and placed them on the coffee table. 'I worked in a pub for over ten years, remember?'

'Oh yeah,' he laughed. 'I didn't know you then, though.'

'Feels like a lifetime ago,' she said with a soft sigh as she caught Michael's eye and he winked at her. They had both been through so much since then, it felt like a lifetime to him too. But he would relive every second of his life over and over with her if he could.

'Just a small one for me, please, Grace,' Stacey insisted, making eyebrows shoot up in surprise and a murmur ripple through the room.

'Something you to have to tell us?' Danny asked as he looked at her and Luke pointedly.

'What?' She blinked before she blushed as the penny dropped, causing Luke to laugh softly. 'I have to be up early, that's all,' she insisted. 'You lot are so nosey anyway.'

'There are no secrets in this family, Stacey. You should know that by now,' Connor said.

'Well, there is no secret,' she insisted.

'Why does Luke look so smug then?' Jake asked with a wicked smirk.

Stacey looked at him with a frown on her face. 'He doesn't. Luke!'

He shook his head at her. 'I'm not doing anything, babe.'

'I am not pregnant!' she insisted.

'Prove it,' Danny challenged her. 'I mean, we're all getting shit-faced tonight, so you'll be the only sober one here. What you got to get up early for anyway?'

Stacey rolled her eyes. 'Work.'

'I'll have a word with your boss and get you the day off,' Danny said, making everyone laugh.

'Can Stacey have the day off?' he asked Jake.

'What's in it for me?'

Danny leaned down and whispered in his ear before Jake spoke again. 'You can have the whole fucking week off if you want, Stace,' he said and even she laughed at that.

Michael sat beside Grace as she lined up the glasses and he poured everyone a generous measure of their best brandy. It was only when everyone had a drink in their hand that Grace addressed the room. 'So, Milo Savage?' she asked.

'Won't be bothering us again,' Connor answered as he wrapped a protective arm around Jazz.

'And is there anyone connected to him that might cause any further trouble?'

'No,' Jake replied. 'No one even knew where he was. Any contacts he had in the past have all died or moved on to different things. That was why he needed Grosvenor's help to get out of the country.'

'Good,' Grace said with a nod before she took a sip of her brandy. 'And our other problem?' she asked, referring to John Barrow – the man who'd had her good friend Nudge killed just so that his former colleagues might dig up some dirt on her family.

'No longer an issue,' Connor assured her.

'So Johnson came through?' Michael asked.

'Yep. Almost makes me glad we kept him around,' Jake said with a grin.

'Well, now that he's proven his worth, maybe we'll keep him around a little longer,' Connor agreed.

'Any other threats on the horizon?' Grace asked as she surveyed the faces in the room.

'None that we know of,' Connor replied.

'Things are looking good,' Jake added. 'And now we have the DI of the Major Incident Team owing us a favour too.'

'Yes,' Grace said with a sigh. 'But let's hope we don't need one any time soon, eh?'

'I think we should drink to that,' Michael said as he raised his glass and everyone else in the room followed suit. 'To calmer times ahead for us all,' he declared and they all voiced their agreement.

Chapter Forty-Two

Grace poured two large glasses of Chardonnay from the ice-cold bottle before returning it to the fridge. Then she carried the drinks into the sitting room where her guest was waiting for her. Leigh Moss looked up from her phone and smiled as Grace handed her the glass and took a seat on the opposite end of the sofa. It had been a shock when Leigh had turned up asking if Grace had time for a chat. Michael had rolled his eyes when the detective had walked into the room and declared he was going to bath the kids. So while he was upstairs doing exactly that, Grace was wondering what bombshell Leigh was about to drop.

'So, what did you want to talk to me about?' Grace asked before taking a sip of her wine.

Leigh sighed softly before she replied. 'I just wanted to talk to someone who might… I don't have many people I can trust. I suppose I just wanted someone who might understand where I was coming from to listen to me.' She shook her head in frustration.

Grace felt a twinge of sympathy for her. Leigh had spent the last twenty years so committed to her job that outside of it she had little else. At least until recently. 'What about John?' she asked.

Leigh took a drink and stared at her. 'I can't talk to him about it because he won't want to influence me. I don't want him to influence me either. I need to do this for me.'

'Oh? So, tell me, what is it you're thinking of doing?' Grace asked although she suspected she already knew the answer.

'I have an idea,' she said and suddenly her eyes were sparkling.

'What kind of idea?' Grace asked with a frown.

'One that I hope you can help me with.'

Grace put down her empty wine glass and sat back against the sofa cushions. She had to give it to Leigh, she had given her idea a lot of thought. According to her, it was something she'd been thinking about for years, but she was missing one crucial component – money. And that was where Grace came in.

'I have to admit, you have my interest piqued,' Grace said as she ran through some of the calculations in her head. It could be a good tax write-off – at least that would be how she would sell it to the rest of the family, not that she thought they would disagree anyway. But actually Grace was convinced that what Leigh had in mind was necessary and long overdue. She sat on her sofa, staring at the wall and trying to think of reasons not to give Leigh the backing that she'd asked for.

'I'm going to hand my resignation in tomorrow anyway,' Leigh said with a determined nod of her head. 'I'm doing this thing one way or another.'

'But you can get it done faster with my money?' Grace said, arching an eyebrow.

Leigh drew her breath. 'Yes, but it's not just that, Grace. I came to you because you know what it feels like to be alone and vulnerable too. I know what you are to the outside world, and although it took me a long time to admit, I also see the woman who would do anything for someone in need. Not to mention, you are a pretty incredible businesswoman. I want you to be a part of this, Grace. Not just because of your money.'

Grace narrowed her eyes at Leigh. They had had so many ups and downs in their long history, but one thing Leigh had never done was blow smoke up her arse. She didn't think the woman even had it in her to be that fake.

'I'll speak to Michael, but I will give it serious thought,' she said.

Leigh smiled. A genuine one. 'Thank you.'

After Leigh had left and their children were in bed, Michael poured the remainder of the wine and handed Grace a fresh glass before sitting beside her with his own. He wrapped his free arm around her shoulder and she leaned into him, nestling her head into the crook of his arm and smiling in contentment.

'So what did Detective Moss want?' he asked with a soft chuckle. 'Your blessing to marry John or something?'

Grace nudged him in the ribs. 'Stop it,' she said, shaking her head and feigning annoyance. 'Actually she had a business proposal for me.'

That made him laugh harder. 'Fuck off! For you?'

'Yep. She's leaving the force.'

He looked down at her, a frown on his handsome features. 'Really?'

'Really.' She took a sip of her wine.

'So what was this business proposal of hers? She getting into the security game or something?' He chuckled again.

'Will you stop?' She laughed now too. 'Actually, it's something I'm really interested in.'

'Really?'

'Really.'

He pulled her closer and she felt the soft groan rumble through his chest. 'I suppose you'd better tell me all about it then.'

John was cooking when Leigh finally arrived at his house a little after 8.30.

'You're late, Detective,' he said with a grin as he slung a tea towel over his shoulder.

She smiled at the sight. An open bottle of Bud on the counter. A pile of chopped peppers and onions on the chopping board and a packet of fresh pasta beside them. John enjoyed cooking and he made simple but delicious food. He was traditionally a meat-and-potatoes kind of man, but he'd been experimenting a little lately and Leigh wasn't about to complain. She had never had anyone look after her the way that John did.

'Can all that wait for a few minutes? I have something to talk to you about,' she said. Her chat with Grace had left her feeling excited and pumped in a way she hadn't felt in years. She was so giddy, she could barely think about eating. Grace had told her that she'd have to speak to Michael, but Leigh already knew that he would support any venture that his wife wanted to go along with, and Leigh could also tell that Grace was interested in her proposal. She hadn't lied when she'd said that she wanted more than just Grace's money; she really believed that the woman could bring so much more to the project than that.

Leigh was desperate to talk to John about it. For the first time in as long as she could remember, she was excited about the future, and this man standing right in front of her was going to be such a big part of that... at least she hoped he would be, anyway.

'Is everything okay?' he asked as he took a few steps toward her.

'Yes.' She nodded vigorously. 'More than okay.' She pulled a chair out from the table. 'Can we just sit for a few minutes?'

John eyed her warily, but then he pulled up a chair too and they both sat at the table.

'First of all, I've decided to leave the force,' Leigh said.

John blew out a breath and ran a hand over his jaw. 'Wow.'

'I know it seems sudden, but you know I've been thinking about this for a while.'

'Yeah… but are you sure, Leigh? This is your career we're talking about.'

'I know that, John, but I've given so much of my life to the force…' She shook her head, suddenly doubting herself.

He reached across the table and took her hand in his, squeezing it reassuringly. 'You don't have to do this for me. I can walk away from my old life, if that's what you need.'

'This isn't for you, John. This is something I want to do for myself. I mean, I'm not going to lie, I'd like you to leave that life behind too, but I'll love you whether you do or not. I know it's a part of who you are.'

'Like being a detective is part of who you are?' he asked with a frown.

'I have loved being a police officer, but I want to do… more.'

'More?'

'You know how frustrated I get with all the red tape and

the bureaucracy… I want to help people without any of that getting in the way.'

'So, you're going to become some kind of vigilante, is that it?' he asked with a wicked grin.

'No.' She smiled back at him. 'I'm going to do something even better and your boss is going to back me.'

'Grace?' He frowned, because as much as he worked for the boys now, Grace was always his boss as far as he was concerned.

'Yes.' Leigh smiled triumphantly before remembering that it wasn't a done deal yet. 'Well, she probably is, but I'm doing it anyway.'

John leaned forward, his elbows on the table and his chin resting on his hands. 'So, what are the two of you planning on doing together then?'

'We're opening a centre for survivors of domestic abuse,' she said, feeling a surge of pride warming her chest.

'Like a refuge?' he asked, his eyes narrowed as he stared across the table at her.

'Kind of, but more. We'll have a centre providing a drop-in service, counselling, expert advice, a surgery of services. And then across the city we'll have a number of self-contained flats for women and children who are fleeing abusive situations. I'm thinking of a dozen to start with.'

'Sounds like you've given this a lot of thought.'

'I have. I've been thinking about it for years. And this is just the start, John. With mine and Grace's contacts combined, we can secure services and funding that will allow us to help as many people as possible. Who knows, we could even set up other similar centres across the country. With budget cuts always affecting the weakest in society, they need all the help they can get. So why not use Grace's business contacts to get money from the private sector too?'

John sat in silence as he digested the information.

'What do you think?' Leigh eventually asked. Although she hated to admit it, she wanted his approval too.

'I think it's a brilliant idea,' he said with a smile. 'And if it makes you happy, then I'm all in. Just let me know what I can do to help.'

'You might just regret that,' she said, pushing her chair back and walking around the table to him.

He pulled her onto his lap, making her squeal. 'I'm sure you'll make it worth my while, Detective,' he said as he nuzzled her neck.

'You can't call me that anymore,' she laughed.

He stopped kissing her and looked into her eyes with such intensity that it made her stomach do a little somersault. 'What shall I call you instead then?'

'What would you like to call me?' she whispered.

'How about my wife?' He arched an eyebrow at her.

Leigh felt like the breath had been sucked from her lungs. Was he serious? Her? Marrying him? 'John, are y-you…?' she stammered.

'Would it freak you out and make you run for the hills if I did?'

'No,' she admitted. 'At least, not if you ask me one day in the future, when we know each other a little better and you've seen me on a Monday morning when we've run out of coffee.'

He kissed her softly. 'I've seen you on a Friday night when we've run out of wine. I'm pretty sure I can cope with any version of you.'

She smiled against his lips.

'But I can wait,' he went on.

'I love you,' she whispered.

He wrapped his giant arms around her. 'I love you too, Detective.'

Epilogue

Twelve months later

Grace Carter leaned against the bar and looked around the room. Oscar was chasing his sister Belle and their cousin Isla around the dancefloor, weaving their way between the legs of the adults who were dancing along to a song that she had never heard before. Connor was twirling Jazz and she was giggling, her face flushed from the dancing and the champagne. Jake and Danny were sitting together in a corner, heads close together, apparently deep in conversation. Whatever they were talking about was making them smile.

'What are you smiling about?' Michael whispered in her ear as he came up beside her, sliding his arm around her waist.

'Them. All of them,' she said with a contented sigh.

'They all look pretty happy,' he agreed as he pulled her closer and then the two of them stood together, watching their children and their extended family. After the whole situation with Isla, there had been a shift in their family. Jazz in particular had some great ideas about new legitimate business ventures for the Cartel Securities empire, and, to Grace's surprise, Jake and Connor had been very open to the idea of making the business entirely legitimate. After the terrifying ordeal of his daughter being kidnapped, Jake had been keen to do anything that would make his family less of a target. And the realisation that it could have just as easily been Paul who was taken seemed to have affected Connor in much the same way. Thankfully, her granddaughter hadn't been too shaken by her ordeal. Sandra, it seemed, had at least been kind to Isla after she had stolen her from them.

Grace wondered if the other woman had truly believed that she had a chance of stealing Jake's child and starting a new life somewhere, hoping that one day Isla might just stop asking where her real family were. The woman had been unhinged. Grace thought about how the years of loneliness and rejection had shaped her into the woman she had become. It had all started with Nathan when Sandra was just eighteen and she had been young and naïve, if not entirely innocent. He had crushed her and walked away, thinking no more of it. That was what he did best. He took hope and love and everything good, and he used it to destroy the people around him. He tossed people away like they were disposable handkerchiefs. Using them until they were no longer of any value to him before tossing them aside and moving on to the next one.

Grace took a sip of her wine and blinked back a tear. It wasn't just Sandra's story that had started with Nathan. Hers had too. She had been eighteen when she met him. Stupid. Gullible. Blinded by love and his incredible smile. He had taken her and used her too – over and over again. Trying his best to destroy everything good in her life. But instead of crumbling, every time he'd tried to break her, she'd come back stronger. She had fought harder and longer and finally beaten him at his own game. She had beaten them all. She was the one standing here in this room full of the people that she loved. She had crushed everyone who had ever tried to hurt her family and now there was no one left to fight. And she couldn't deny the relief of that was overwhelming. She'd been fighting for over twenty-five years and finally she was looking forward to a slower pace of life.

'You okay?' Michael asked, pressing his lips against her ear and making goosebumps prickle over her skin.

She turned to him and smiled. 'Yes. Just thinking about the past.'

He smiled back at her. 'The past? Weddings are about the future.'

'I know.' She nudged him in the ribs. 'I was thinking about the journey we took to get here. Look at them.' She turned back to the crowd of people packed into the hotel ballroom. 'See how happy they are, Michael?'

'Yeah,' he agreed.

'We did it, didn't we?' she asked as she rested her head on his shoulder. Because this was where it all began – the desire to keep her son Jake safe and happy had led her right here. Into the arms of the man she loved more than she had ever dreamed possible, the man who adored her and made her feel like the most important person in the world, the man who had given her another two children, her stepson, daughter-in-law, grandchildren and the rest of the Carter family. And now here she was at her son's wedding reception. Danny Alexander made Jake happier than Grace had ever seen him before and he was a perfect addition to their family.

'We sure did, love.'

He kissed her on the head and then took her glass of wine out of her hand. 'Dance with me,' he said, taking her hand and pulling her towards the dancefloor.

'I don't know this song,' she protested feebly.

'So?' he shrugged as he kept on walking backwards until they were on the dancefloor beside Jazz and Connor.

'Oh, watch out. The old man is up,' Connor laughed as he and Jazz made a little room.

'Less of the old, son,' Michael said with a fake scowl.

A few moments later, Jake and Danny were beside them too and the opening bars of 'Titanium' started to play.

'Now, I know you know this one,' Michael said with a grin.

'I sure do,' she laughed and then he wrapped her in his arms and kissed her. She was vaguely aware of their adult children groaning and making fake vomiting noises beside them, but she didn't care.

She was Grace Carter.

She was titanium.

Acknowledgments

As always, I would like to thank the wonderful team at One More Chapter for believing in me and bringing these books to life, most especially Charlotte Ledger and Kim Young whose support of The Bad Blood series has helped it go from strength to strength. I'd also love to thank my amazing editor, Jennie Rothwell for championing the Carters and helping to shape the stories of the next generation. Your advice and support has been invaluable to me.

Most of all, I'd love to thank all of the readers who have supported me and who have bought or read my books. You have made my dreams come true.

I couldn't do this without the support of other authors too, and the crime writing community are a particularly lovely and supportive group of people. But, I'd like to give a special mention to Mary Torjussen and Amanda Brooke, for always being willing to lend a listening ear and for putting up with me and my Monday night ramblings. I would be lost without you both.

To all of my friends who put up with my constant writing chatter. There are too many to mention, and I love you all! A huge thank-you to my family for their constant love and support.

Read on for an extract from Payback Time...

IF YOU CHALLENGE THE CARTERS

Connor Carter and Jake Conlon are having trouble with a rival gang, and it's clear they've underestimated their power. But no son of the infamous Grace Carter is going to let someone else run the streets of Liverpool.

YOU MUST BE PREPARED TO FIGHT

Then Jake's right-hand man Danny Alexander is arrested for murder and remanded in custody. The cartel know he's innocent but the evidence is overwhelmingly against him. The Carters alliance with DI Leigh Moss has always been fragile but it's time to put aside their differences if they want to find the real killer…

Prologue

Former Chief Superintendent John Barrow lay back on his bunk with his hands behind his head.

'You all set for tomorrow?' he asked his pad-mate lying on the bunk above.

'Yeah. I can't fucking wait,' he replied with a contented sigh.

'And you remember everything we discussed?'

'Of course, John. We've gone over it half a dozen times. I'll make sure that things go according to plan. The wheels are already in motion. Don't worry.'

Barrow smiled to himself. He was facing life in prison with no chance of parole for another twenty-four years because of that bitch Grace Carter and her gang of thugs. The Carters were the scum of the earth as far as he was concerned, and he couldn't wait for the day when they were finally brought to their knees. They had ruled Liverpool for far too long and it was about time for a changing of the guard. To his disgust, most of his colleagues and former friends had disowned him when he'd been arrested for murder and child sexual exploitation. People were hypocrites. Nobody had given a thought to the kind of women and girls he'd sought the services of when they were alive. That was how people like him had been able to prey on them so easily and for so long. But he still had enough contacts, and enough dirt on enough people, to be able to pull some strings – even from the confines of his cell in HMP Wymott.

The thing with prisoners like him was that they were all put on a wing together for their own protection. *Vulnerable prisoners.* So, when he bumped into a former associate of his, it wasn't a huge surprise. But it was a stroke of luck that this particular associate had a reason to hate the Carters just as much as he did. Well, one Carter in particular. The man who had stolen the love of his life – at least, that was what his pad-mate believed anyway. And John Barrow wasn't about to point out the sheer stupidity of doing anything for the love of a woman when it wasn't going to serve his own ends. He didn't care what his associates' motives were, he only cared that they shared a common goal – bringing down the Carters. If it hadn't been for their interfering in something that had fuck-all to do with them, he wouldn't be sitting in this tiny, stinking cell.

Since he was an ex-copper, most of the screws hated Barrow as much as the cons did, but there were some who recognised the authority and power he still held, and they treated him well. He was able to ensure that he and his old friend were padded up together, and with nothing but time on their hands, they had spent the last six months plotting the downfall of the Carter empire.

'Don't underestimate this new crew,' Barrow warned. 'They might be feral, but they are ruthless and not quite as stupid as they look.'

'I know the score,' came the reply. 'Stop fretting, John. I promise you that the Carters' days are numbered. I will bring them to their knees, and then I will take back what is rightfully mine.'

'I only wish I could be there to see the arrogant grins wiped off their faces when you do.'

'Hmm,' his cell mate mumbled into the darkness. 'Soon they will all know that *she* belonged to me first.'

Chapter 1

Devlin King's fingers curled around the handle of the Beretta handgun as he stared out of the car window into the darkness. This shooter was the real deal. He'd used guns before plenty of times, but they were converted replicas or antiques and as such they weren't always reliable, as the missing tip of the thumb of his right hand could attest. But this one he held onto now was the dog's bollocks. He and his older brother, Jerrod, had a new benefactor, and while Devlin didn't trust him as much as Jerrod did, he had to admit he had come through for them in getting them four of the finest quality clean handguns Devlin had ever seen in his life in order to pull off this job. And given who they were going up against, they would need to prove that they had the balls and the resources to be contenders for the top spot.

Now the King brothers and two of their most experienced soldiers were sitting in an old Ford Estate on a dark country road somewhere in Scotland, waiting for a shipment of Connor Carter and Jake Conlon's cocaine to be delivered. The brothers had recently come by some new and interesting information about how the drugs were being transported, and it was too good an opportunity to miss out on. They were using a local car-hire firm to transport the goods from the border up to Glasgow, with minimal security. It was easy pickings as far as Devlin was concerned. The thing with Conlon and Carter was that they were a pair of arrogant pricks, and one day it was going to be their downfall. They believed they were untouchable. And while half of the city of Liverpool might shit their pants at the mere mention of their name, Devlin and his brother knew what they were really about. Too interested in looking pretty to get their hands dirty anymore. They sat in their fancy fucking cars and their flash designer suits, looking down at people like him, who knew what it was really like to graft your arse off to get what you want. Conlon and Carter had gone soft and now it was time for the Bridewell Blades to show everyone what they were capable of and step into the limelight for a change.

'Shouldn't he have been past by now?' Jerrod barked from the front seat of the car.

'It's only been ten minutes,' Devlin reminded him.

'We better not have missed them!' Jerrod growled.

'We haven't! Our lads saw the handover. He'll be here,' Devlin snapped. They had two of their men stationed four miles down the road where the drop-off was taking place, and they'd confirmed the drop had gone without incident.

Chapter 1

'Here he is now. A white Renault Mégane, right?'

'That's them,' Jerrod snapped as he opened the car door and jumped out, quickly followed by the other three men. It was Jerrod who fired the first shot at the car, causing it to veer off the road and straight into a ditch.

The four men ran to the car. Devlin peered inside to see the driver slumped over the wheel with blood pouring from his head. He was either dead or unconscious. Devlin pointed the gun at the window beside his head. He may as well make sure, he thought to himself.

'Dev!' Jerrod shouted, full of excitement. 'We have hit the fucking jackpot here, kid! Come on. Give us a hand?'

Devlin lowered his gun and jogged to the back of the car where his brother and their two associates had forced open the boot to reveal four black holdalls full of cocaine. Devlin smiled at the sight as they lifted the bags from the car. This stuff had to be worth a fucking fortune, and if it was good-quality gear, they could cut it with something else and double their profits.

'Come on, before someone sees something and phones the bizzies,' Jerrod snapped again, breaking Devlin from his daze, as he was already thinking of the new motor he was going to buy himself. He took a holdall from his brother and the four ran back over the road to their own car, stashing the four black bags beneath the back seat before jumping inside. Adrenaline thundered around Devlin's body as the driver started the engine and sped off down the narrow country road.

'How fucking easy was that, lads?' Jerrod laughed

loudly and the rest of them joined in. The atmosphere in the car sizzled with excitement and electricity as they congratulated each other on a job well done.

'Big things are about to happen for us,' Jerrod went on excitedly. 'Those pretentious pricks aren't going to know what's hit them.'

'Too fucking right!' Devlin agreed with a vigorous nod of his head. They hadn't needed the shooters in the end, which only proved to him further that he and his brother didn't need anyone but themselves and their loyal soldiers.

Devlin leaned back against the seat and smiled to himself. Jerrod was right. Big things were about to happen for them. He could feel it in his bones.

Payback Time **is available in paperback and ebook now**

The Bad Blood Series

All titles available now in ebook and paperback

The Bad Blood Series

YOUR NUMBER ONE STOP

ONE MORE CHAPTER

FOR PAGETURNING BOOKS

One More Chapter is an
award-winning global
division of HarperCollins.

Sign up to our newsletter to get our
latest eBook deals and stay up to date
with our weekly Book Club!
<u>Subscribe here.</u>

Meet the team at
<u>www.onemorechapter.com</u>

Follow us!

🐦 <u>@OneMoreChapter_</u>
f <u>@OneMoreChapter</u>
📷 <u>@onemorechapterhc</u>

Do you write unputdownable fiction?
We love to hear from new voices.
Find out how to submit your novel at
<u>www.onemorechapter.com/submissions</u>